Bridge Below the Belt

by

Larry Cohen & Liz Davis

Natco Press 1997

Cover design by Jude Goodwin-Hanson

Bridge Below the Belt

by

Larry Cohen & Liz Davis

Edited by Arthur Jacobs

Thanks to:

Tim Bourke, Susie Cohen, Leta & Rufus Davis,
Jim Houser, John Lewis, Alex McCallum,
Ravindra Murthy and Naomi Sachs

SPECIAL THANKS to Paul Cohen, Karen McCallum
and Steve Weinstein

Copyright ©1997 by Natco Press

ISBN No. 0-9634715-5-4
Library of Congress Catalog Card Number: 97-091842

Table of Contents

The Players

The Majors:

<u>Hereford Willis III:</u> Past 60, but powerfully built, and with more oil wells than scruples; spite, sarcasm, ruthlessness and an unforgiving nature are some of his more pleasant qualities.

<u>Parson:</u> Hereford's hired bridge pro. Not restricted by ethics or personal hygiene.

<u>Vanessa (The Contessa):</u> Unpleasant and untalented, she owns Miami's new upscale bridge club, Trumps, and would also like to own . . .

<u>Ford Maddox:</u> A brilliant professional player and Hereford's bitter enemy. Closing in on 40, he's known for his puckish charm and gracious demeanor. He shares a secret.

The Minors:

<u>Meyer:</u> Ford's first bridge partner and long-time pal, a private detective who is reliable and loyal to his friends.

<u>Penny:</u> Bridge director and programmer, she's thirty-something, attractive, decent, but unlucky. She desperately hopes that the mistakes of her carefree college days don't return to haunt her.

<u>Richie:</u> Longtime friend of Penny's; inveterate gambler and proprietor of the run-down Aces bridge club; can he make a new start?

The Ladies of the Club:

Maura: A good player, much in demand in her circle; she has a constitution of steel and a fascination with the world of disease.

Prissy: Happy to play with a partner as good as Maura; desperately looking for her own moment in the sun at the local bridge club.

Eileen: At 68, she still has the voracious appetite of two lumberjacks and a sense of humor to match.

Gilda: Eternally consumed with her possessions, her status and herself.

Heavy Hearts

The wind flew through the summer sky, pelting Miami with warm rain. Wearing a cap of gray curls and matching steel-rimmed glasses, Maura Bund watched the storm through her front window as she awaited Priscilla, her bridge partner.

On Maura's fortieth birthday, some hundred years earlier, she had become acutely preoccupied with her mortality. An intelligent woman, her friends quickly came to know her as a veritable encyclopedia of disease. Over a cup of tea, she could speak eloquently on the subject of small intestines or work herself into a rapture about the colon. And nothing made her eyes twinkle like the discussion of bowel movements. The size, shape, consistency, and color all revealed a person's state of health or lack thereof. Interpreting bowel movements was a fine art, and Maura read them as finely as a gifted fortune teller read tea-leaves.

She could tell you what disease was most likely lurking nearby (she experienced all the symptoms regularly, and could easily spot them in others). Today, for instance, would be ripe for contracting pneumonia. The thick, phlegmy, tropical air was loaded with pollutants headed straight for your lungs. The rain was falling so hard it would soak you to the bone. And as Maura was headed for the bridge club for her weekly game, she would be sitting at a table all day while air conditioners froze her bones—everything you need for pneumonia. In preparation for venturing out, Maura reached down and cinched the belt on her raincoat ever tighter, hoping to ward off the unruly advances of the grasping wet wind. By the time Priscilla's silver Mercedes pulled up, Maura's mind had slipped into replaying one of her favorite death fantasies. When she wasn't concentrating on symptoms, she frequently imagined her own death filled with drama and poignancy. The ominous din of the storm was the perfect backdrop for Maura's daydream. She saw herself heroically walking to the car, being struck down by lightning, and being taken away in an ambulance. After imagining her death, her mind flashed to the wake. She saw her friends gathered around her casket, mourning the quiet greatness of her modest (but heroic) life. Maura had at least one death fantasy a day. While they all shared an identical ending, Maura found it profoundly satisfying to vary the Death's *modus operandi*. She did not recall whether she had ever been struck by lightning before. This might be a first.

Priscilla Bristlemore proudly parked her sleek new car in front of Maura's house. It had a fine interior, complete with supple black leather and mahogany trim. This was Prissy's pride and joy—she loved her car above all else. It *was* who she *was*. Prissy flipped down the driver's side sun visor and clicked on the bright little vanity light. She checked her deep, rich, burgundy lipstick. The palette of her make-up was skillfully matched with the hue of her dyed sable hair. Unfortunately for Prissy, her lovely, soft, 70-year-old skin had not also been dyed to match. The combination of white skin and deep lipstick was startling, if you weren't prepared for it. Prissy did not yet understand the silver luminosity of graceful age.

The horn honked loudly. Maura dragged herself out of her daydream and braced for the soggy journey from the house to the car. Giving her belt the last cinch, she turtled her head into her collar and carefully navigated the walk. Priscilla pushed the car door open, knowing Maura's frail arms would struggle with it. The car door hung in the rain. Every raindrop within a ten-mile radius found its way into the open silver door. By the time Maura got to the car, the seat was drenched, the carpet was soaked, and the dashboard had trickles of rain dripping to the floorboard. Priscilla frantically mopped up the seat with an old towel, grumbling under her breath.

"Maura! For Heaven's sake, get in and close the door!" Prissy scolded.

Maura sat on the seat, gathered her legs in after herself, and placed both her hands on the door handle. She pulled. The door didn't move. The rain fell. "Maura, close the door!" Prissy yelled.

Maura let out a big breath and pulled the door closed. She peered out from under her dripping raincoat. "Whew, I made it. It's dangerous out there," she said. "You know, I could have been hit by lightning," she pointed out, "and in my condition I'm especially susceptible to electric shock."

Prissy rolled her eyes and sighed futilely. "Well then, what took you so long?" she said, her voice weary with exasperation. Maura strapped herself into the car seat like an astronaut about to be catapulted into space and Prissy sped off for the bridge game.

"Prissy," Maura raised her eyebrows and paused for effect, "remember, the tortoise won the race."

Priscilla squinted through her glasses. She had received many compliments on these lenses, because although they were bifocals, the line was not apparent. It was a much younger look, Prissy thought. They chattered all the way to the club. For all of Maura's annoying idiosyncracies, and imaginary ailments, she *was* one of the best bridge players at the club. And winning was very important to Prissy. She would gladly trade listening to Maura talk about some disease, or morosely ponder her own death, for the satisfaction of winning at the club. Prissy had evaluated this trade-off frequently.

By the time they got to the club, most of the other regulars were already there. Eileen Gready hovered territorially around the luncheon food next to the coffee machine. She greeted Maura and Prissy between mouthfuls of spinach dip which she had slathered on an unsuspecting slice of bread.

"Hello there, ladies," she said, sending out food-laden spittle like a goodwill messenger. "Nice weather," she added with a laugh that revealed her personal favorites from the luncheon selection. Prissy answered with a limp smile that fell short of disguising her disgust. Eileen turned and steered her graying bulk toward the far end of the food counter. Prissy immediately checked her crisp linen lapels for food particles. "That woman eats like she plays bridge. She hogs everything," said Prissy distastefully.

"Yes, she is a hand-hog, isn't she?" Maura reflected.

"She certainly is. Eileen steals every hand she possibly can. I don't know how Gilda can stand it."

"I would not like to play with her," Maura confirmed. "She thinks she plays better than anyone else."

"Yes. I don't know why she feels she has to declare all the hands. Gilda is a pretty good player." Priscilla had a hard time imagining playing with Eileen.

"Yes, she is a good player," Maura said after consideration. "But she's too flashy. She tries to make the showy play, even when it's not there," Maura pinpointed her own thoughts.

"Maura, my hair has completely wilted from the humidity and the rain, and you know how that bothers me. I must go freshen up before game time; otherwise, I'll never be able to concentrate on anything," Prissy stated. She drew up the well-groomed bearing of her seventy years, head high, chin tucked, glasses perched, and strode regally to the bathroom. She did not look in need of freshening.

Maura methodically made her way to the teapot. She believed many foods led to a premature death, so, despite her doctor's assurances of good health, she had placed herself on a very restricted diet. At the club, she drank decaffeinated tea, lukewarm. She was slowly carrying her tea to the table when she heard the bold laugh of Gilda Shein reverberating through the bridge club. Gilda passed out her Hollywood kisses like invitations to a large, but still exclusive, gala. Midway through the procession her diamond bracelet snagged someone's sweater, which prompted a comedy of errors involving everybody's jewelry getting caught on everybody's clothing. This performance offered the perfect opportunity for the communal comparison of gems, gold and the occasional strand of pearls. Gilda shone brightly under the hot light of envy; each plump, milky hand swathed in translucent rocks and shiny metal.

The din began to die down and Gilda, not wanting to leave the spotlight just yet, reached into her handbag and withdrew a newspaper clipping. Raising it into the air like a speaker's wine glass, she proclaimed, "Wait till you see this amazing hand! Has anyone seen this hand? It happened Saturday at the sectional, and *I* was there." She smoothed the clipping out onto the table so all could see the hand, and began to read,

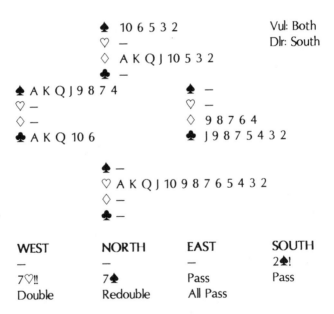

			Vul: Both
♠ 10 6 5 3 2			Dlr: South
♡ —			
◇ A K Q J 10 5 3 2			
♣ —			

♠ A K Q J 9 8 7 4　　　　♠ —
♡ —　　　　　　　　　　♡ —
◇ —　　　　　　　　　　◇ 9 8 7 6 4
♣ A K Q 10 6　　　　　　♣ J 9 8 7 5 4 3 2

♠ —
♡ A K Q J 10 9 8 7 6 5 4 3 2
◇ —
♣ —

WEST	NORTH	EAST	SOUTH
—	—	—	2♠!
7♡!!	7♠	Pass	Pass
Double	Redouble	All Pass	

At last weekend's sectional in Miami, a famous hand somehow found its way into the tournament. When the South players on Board Four picked up their cards, they received the

14

shock of a lifetime. Most simply opened the bidding with seven hearts and were disappointed to hear West overcall seven spades. Some of the North's doubled, and all around the room North-South were plus either 100 or 200.

The very same deal, right down to the last spot card, originally appeared in the classic bridge book, *Right Through the Pack*, by Robert Darvas. In the fictitious story, the bidding followed the unbelievable sequence shown in the auction diagram. The South player, an ``inveterate psycher,'' opened the South hand with a strong two bid in SPADES! He figured that he'd sneak up on the opponents and end up getting doubled in seven hearts. West played a joke of his own by jumping to seven HEARTS! If he got doubled he planned to run to seven SPADES. Meanwhile, this ``counter-psyche'' had the effect of eliciting a seven-spade call from North! West doubled and North redoubled. West, suspecting that all the missing spades were in dummy, led the spade seven. Declarer played low from dummy, and went on to lose all thirteen tricks. He was down 13 doubled and redoubled minus 100 honors for à loss of a record 7700 points.

It was not known how this famous deal could appear as a computer-generated hand in the tournament. According to the *Encyclopedia of Bridge*, the odds of this occurring are 1 in 52,644,737,765,488,792,839,237,440,000. League officials are investigating.

Immediately the women's voices sparked the fire of controversy, each person offering an explanation for the appearance of the hand at the tournament. The speculations popped and crackled amidst the electric hum of hand analysis. Priscilla came back from the powder room looking, ironically, exactly the same as she had when she went in. She fluttered over to the excitement and alighted near Gilda's shoulder. Prissy looked down and gulped, "I think I would faint if I picked up 13 of a suit. Did you actually play this, Gilda?" she asked, with a new admiration for her friend.

"I did. When *I* played it," Gilda beamed beneath her perfectly coifed silver wig, "I opened seven hearts." She waited for the women to coo at such a gutsy bid (rarely did anybody actually open at the seven level). "West doubled me," she narrated theatrically, sending a buzz through the crowd, "and I made 2470 *for a top!*" Gilda's pride bubbled out of every pore. Her friends showered her with congratulations, and quickly returned to wondering how that hand had come up in the sectional. Prissy walked over to her partner and said, "Maura, I'm not sure I understand that story from *Right Through the Pack*. Why would anyone open two spades with 13 hearts?"

"Oh, well, the guy with the hearts was trying to trick the other fellow. He wanted to get doubled in seven hearts. But his opponent, West, was a gambler with a sense of humor. So he bid the heart suit as a joke. The bidding went around, and eventually it paid off for West," Maura chuckled to herself.

"Imagine, plus 7700," Prissy said foggily, starry-eyed.

"Yes, imagine. There's something funny about that hand showing up in the sectional. Mark my words, it's not natural," Maura's heavy heart dragged her voice low.

"Oh Maura," Prissy teased lightly, "it's just a coincidence. Have some fun."

Fired

It was 11 o'clock—a humid Memphis Monday morning. Dazed, Penny stood for a long time in the doorway of the old brick office building. Absently, she began using her thumbnail to pick off the dingy white paint hanging from the door frame. She continued to work, peeling the paint off in long strips. With each strip her mind quieted, until she was working rhythmically, chipping and peeling the old paint off the frame. She used her key to scrape the patches that clung to the door, freeing them to scatter themselves on the doorstep. What delight she felt to see the many layers of paint revealed: a greasy yellow peering through, an old colonial brown below it. Her hands, sticky with sweat, would occasionally sweep over her work, whisking away any of the white paint flecks that lingered.

A newly-pressed man in creamy linen pants sauntered by. Penny looked up to meet his glance and was startled to see his fascinated stare of disgust. She had been so absorbed in chipping the paint from the door frame that she had forgotten herself. The tattered cardboard boxes and plastic bags that held the remnants of her personal belongings spilled onto the sidewalk. Her rumpled dress hung limply from her shoulders, not quite camouflaging her attractive frame. Teary make-up streaked down the soft cheeks of her puffy, but pleasing face. She was debuting, this bright Monday morning, as a bag lady in the street vignette of life. As Penny saw herself through the eyes of the passerby, she laughed out loud. For him, this was the final confirmation of her madness: he fled.

Slightly disoriented in her unexpected freedom, Penny giggled to herself as she pulled the car around to the front of the National Bridge League's office building. Packing the boxes into the car, she noticed she had no attachment to them at all. They were of no more use to her than the discarded flakes of chipped paint. She wondered how she could feel so much nothing about the passing of a job that had occupied the last ten years of her life. But by the time she pulled into the parking lot of her apartment building, the giddiness of her new-found freedom had been eclipsed by a very aggressive army of anxiety. Rent, food, car insurance, and electricity always make a house feel like a home. Her chest tightened. She needed a plan, and quick. Wasting no time, she zipped upstairs, grabbed a Diet Pepsi from the fridge, and called her trustworthy friend Meyer in Florida.

"Meyer here," the voice was firm and resolute. It had the professional effect of private investigators who were movie buffs. It worked for Meyer.

"Meyer? It's me, Penny. How are you?" she said, coercing her voice into cheerfulness. Given the circumstances, cheerfulness would have been a difficult feat for a contortionist.

Not only had Meyer and Penny once worked together at the National Bridge League, but they had remained close pals and cohorts ever since. He knew her like the back of his proverbial hand. That, combined with his investigative acumen and general intuition, led him to the conclusion that a cracking voice midday Monday could only mean trouble. "Penny? What's going on?" he insisted.

For the second time that day, tears navigated their way down her face. "It's unbelievable, really. I can't believe it. I don't know what happened. I have no idea what happened."

"Just start from the beginning," he coaxed. Meyer, familiar with her bumpy past, did not think he had ever heard her this upset.

"I'll try to be brief," she stammered.

"Take your time. Details are my business," he reassured her.

Penny blotted her eyes, then sat down with her Pepsi. "Basically, it was a horrible day from the beginning. Some guy had my car blocked in, and that put me behind schedule about forty-five minutes. When I finally got to work, I raced to my desk to check my voice mail as I booted up my computer. You remember our boss, Ms. Dowl?"

"Outstanding in her uniqueness. The only person I have ever known to have absolutely no life outside of the office." Meyer had always been curious about Ms. Dowl's motivation for living.

"Yeah, well, nothing has changed. She is at the office before anyone, leaves after everyone, and doesn't take lunch or go to the bathroom. I don't know how she does it."

"Some kind of esoteric training, I think. So what happened? You got in and—," Meyer prompted.

"So my voice mail is echoing with her voice, as stern and cold as it gets, 'requesting a private meeting as soon as you get in.' I went in. I assumed she was angry because I was late, and I was prepared to explain what had happened. She asks me if I'd like to sit down and I, of course, say no thank you. She then says, 'I think you'd better have a seat.' I sat. I was thinking at the time, I can't believe she's making such a big deal out of

19

this lateness. I'm hardly ever late. She asked me what happened over the weekend.

"I really didn't understand what she was saying. I wondered if she was trying to be social in some strange way, but she was far too serious for that. Then I thought, okay, she's trying out a new management style. You know, in the last ten years I've said maybe five words to her a year, and two of them are 'Merry Christmas.' I assumed she was trying to be more personal, but didn't quite know how to break the ice. So, in a friendly way, I told her that I don't work on the weekends and I didn't know if anything much happened here on the weekend. Then I asked her if I had inadvertently missed a deadline, or a meeting.

"She stared at me silently like I was a criminal. It seemed like she stared at me for a very long time, silent. She just sat there, rigid, staring right through me. I swear she didn't blink once. It was as though she just found out I was the shooter in the Kennedy assassination. Meanwhile, by some inexplicable process, I actually became embarrassed, as though I had been caught doing something terribly wrong. I still had no idea what it was, mind you, but it was certainly horrific. I must have committed a heinous crime while sleepwalking.

"So by this time, I am sitting there on a hard chair feeling like a schoolgirl, queasy and faint with dread. Just as I am ready to throw up or pass out or both, she says, like she's announcing the death of the President, 'Someone broke into the computer.' I've got to tell you Meyer, after enduring all the ominous drama of this tension-filled scene that was pervaded with mystery and scandal, to hear this . . . I almost laughed out loud. I think I coughed or something to try and hide it. The absurdity. I confess—I lost a lot of respect for her right then. All those years of never seeing her or having contact with her; she was always 'The Boss.' And she's having a fit over computer accessing? So someone broke into the computer; it didn't sound too serious to me. It's a bridge league, not the Pentagon defense command. We don't have any inside information of takeover targets, any secret formulas or ad campaigns. Give it a rest.

"I guess I must have been smiling, because she barked at me, 'This is a grave issue of security,' and she pointed her nose in my face. I wanted to laugh again. What security? Someone wants an address list to mail people stuff? A phone list? What, is this the latest fad in serial killing, National Bridge League members? Finally, I look right back at her and I said, 'Ms. Dowl, forgive me, but I really don't understand what's going on. Can you explain?' Oh boy. I asked for it. She asked me if I read the newspaper's daily bridge column. I said, generally, yes, but I haven't today. She said there was a sectional tournament in Miami over the weekend. During the course of play, a very unusual hand came up. A famous hand. At this point, I was still really confused—and to tell you the truth Meyer, I still am confused. The odds of this hand coming up are, and she quoted it but I forgot what she said. Frankly, who would bother to know the odds; they're a gazillion to one."

"As a point of interest, they are exactly the same as the odds of any other hand coming up," Meyer remarked factually.

"It is not remotely a point of interest with me, Meyer, which was my point precisely. Now let me tell the story." *Men and their facts.* Penny continued, "So I said to her, 'Ms. Dowl, I still don't quite understand the ramifications of all this, much less what it has to do with me.' Ms. Dowl, I'm afraid, became something of a piss-pot when I said this. She raised her voice, 'Well it's obvious, isn't it? Someone tampered with the deal generator! There are only three of us who have the password. My boss, myself, and you, Miss McGill. Unfortunately this compromises the integrity of the League. People may think all of our competitions are fixed.' Utterly ludicrous. I stopped listening right about there. She kept talking for some time, but, well, you know how it is when you're getting fired."

"You got fired?" Meyer was shocked.

"Very fired. Evidently, as a lark, some hacker broke into the computer, accessed the deal generator, and put this famous hand in. I don't know. I haven't even heard of the hand." Penny was exasperated. She had been fired for a childish prank. Someone else's childish prank at that. It was ridiculous. "So," she hastened, wanting to discuss the more pressing issues of rent and car insurance, "I need a plan. A big plan for my life, which has just ceased to exist."

"Wait a minute. What was the hand?" Meyer would not be deterred. The scent was hot.

"What do you mean, what was the hand? Who cares? I'm fired because some punk input a hand." Meyer could be annoyingly tangential at times.

"No no no. Maybe we can tell who did it if we know what hand. You said it was famous. Hit me with it; I'll probably know it, or my former bridge partner will."

"All right. Somebody was dealt all 13 hearts, and another guy had eight solid spades, well, almost solid . . ."

"Good God. That *is* a famous hand. It's from

22

Right Through the Pack, by Robert Darvas. It's a fictitious hand, but famous nonetheless." Meyer's brain effortlessly shifted into gear. "Why would somebody choose that hand?" Meyer wondered aloud. "What makes you think it's a kid, Penny?"

"Why not? I mean, what adult would have the time to sit around breaking into people's computers and inputting outrageous hands?" Penny really wanted to get back to the issue, which was her livelihood.

Meyer paused.

"Meyer? Hello? Rent? Money? No job? Plan, Meyer, plan." Penny was losing him.

"The plan . . . hmm. Move here to Miami. You can stay with me in the office . . . er, . . . ah, my guest room. Richie has a bridge club here. Call him up and see if he needs a director. Besides, I can always use help in the investigating business. So the answer is—"

"Answer to what?" Penny interrupted. She wanted to know whether she should really move to Miami.

"To the question of what adult would have time for this. An adult who wanted to make a big splash, but anonymously. So that he or she would have the satisfaction of beating the system, without the notoriety. Someone who doesn't have too much of a home life or social life, so he or she would have the uninterrupted time. Someone who knows computers and likes to play around with them . . ." Meyer was on a roll. Penny knew him too well. To her, this was dallying.

"So Meyer, you're sure I can move in there with you for a while? I don't want to stress the friendship, you know."

"Hmm? Oh yeah. Pack and come on. You will have to do a little rearranging, that's all. I have storage for your furniture and stuff in the garage." Meyer was lost in thought. "Okay. I'll be there. I always did want to see Florida. All those big bugs and slow drivers. I never did like Memphis much anyway." "Especially after getting the ax." Even deep in thought, Meyer could be counted on for a friendly ribbing. "Especially," laughed Penny, acknowledging the truth of that statement. "Thanks again, Meyer." Armed with a plan, she hung up satisfied.

* * * * * * * * * *

A tightly focused pair of steel blue eyes pushed the small white ball as it sailed through the windless azure sky. The ball dropped triumphantly on the green. The eyes, peaceful in success, rested in the chiseled, domineering face of Hereford Willis III. Hereford handed his custom-made titanium four-iron to his caddy and turned gracefully to his guest. "What do you think, Ashenfelter? An astounding day for golfing. This may be the best day all year."

Jon Ashenfelter, fifteen years Hereford's junior, was still admiring the other man's superlative shot. "Yes, I think you're right. This is the best day all year. Very pleasant temperature and low humidity. Quite unusual for Florida." Ashenfelter felt uneasy about his own tee shot. He stepped forward and studied the hole. Pausing, he mentally adjusted his stroke to avoid the difficulty of the bunker on the left side of the green. He walked back to the caddy, took a club, and walked over to the tee box. Teeing his ball up, he sensed an uneasiness in his stomach. They were on the fourth hole, a par three, and this was the first time Hereford had spoken. "Hereford," Ashenfelter turned to face him. "Yes, Jon." Hereford was still air before a tornado. "Hereford, pardon my vulgarity. I've known you a long time, and your reputation longer. I know you do not play golf during the middle of the week because your work is both your pleasure and your obsession. So we are here for business, except that you and I *have* no business together. We only know each other personally as competitors in the bridge world. This is undoubtedly one of the most beautiful and exclusive golf courses in the country and I may never have the opportunity to play it again. Frankly, I would hate to waste it thinking of you. What is it I can do for you today?" Speaking the Unspoken, Ashenfelter had quieted his restless mind. He did not pause now for Hereford's answer. Freed from concern, he lined up at the tee armed with his five-iron. His strong and accurate swing sent the ball onto the green, rolling inside Hereford's extraordinary shot.

Hereford's sonorous laugh wafted on the warm breeze. "Excellent shot!" he called to Ashenfelter. Jon stood a moment, slightly baffled by his own success. But Ashenfelter knew better than to expose himself to such an adversary, and turned to face Hereford with a conqueror's confidence.

Hereford Willis III loved nothing more than tough, solid competition. He smiled appreciatively at Ashenfelter. "Jon," Hereford did not miss a beat, "I want you to fire Ford Maddox." Jon's face fell. The tempest had hit, swift and unexpected.

Jon stammered, "My bridge pro, you mean. That Ford Maddox? Your—"

"Yes. The one and same. Fire him."

"But why? For Chrissake, Hereford, really." Ashenfelter had been completely unnerved. "Is this about winning bridge tournaments? I thought you enjoyed playing against us."

"I do." Hereford's penetrating eyes zeroed in unwaveringly on Jon's. Silence.

Jon shook off the look. "I just can't figure it out. No. No, I won't fire Ford. Not without a really good reason. Why should I?" Ashenfelter was clouded with disbelief.

"The deal you are trying to put together with Pierman Oil?" Hereford queried patiently.

"What about it?" Ashenfelter's mind was spinning. How could Hereford possibly have known about that deal?

"You've almost agreed with them on a price for parcel T4?"

Jon's eyes narrowed and his body tensed.

Hereford resumed, "I have known Dick Pierman for a very long time. I am going to be calling him from the sixth hole to let him know whether to go ahead with your deal. Call Ford. Fire him. The caddy has my phone. Just think, if you call now, you may still birdie this hole. Consider it."

Giving his guest a modicum of privacy, Hereford turned and strolled down the fairway. He was thinking only about his putt. In this moment, he belonged entirely to the challenge of the golf course.

What a sick bastard, Jon Ashenfelter thought as he dialed the cellular phone.

Dialing for Dollars

Hereford Willis III crossed his expansive office and closed the heavy mahogany office door. He strode decisively back to his helm, each socked foot crushing the thick pile of the carpet as an added emphasis to the speech that was playing in his mind. Snatching the phone out of the cradle like a hungry man grabbing up his last foreseeable lamb chop, he dialed his bridge pro, and turned to watch his own reflection in the gilt mirror that hung behind his desk. He was a man of action, and he liked to watch himself in action. He was, he always felt privately, the consummate tycoon, possessing the perfect balance of ruthlessness and the ability to detect human weakness.

He glared at himself menacingly as he waited for the phone pick-up. The answering voice was groggy and irritated; clearly, sleep had been interrupted.

"Hello," accused the sleeping voice.

"Parson? Get your lazy fat ass up outta that mattress! We have work to do." Hereford looked smugly at his reflection. He was about to have the satisfaction of ruining this man's day, and maybe, if he were really lucky, the next year of his life.

Realizing it was his boss on the other end of the line, Parson, the equally consummate bridge pro, paused a moment to collect himself. "Hereford," the formerly agitated voice was now as sweet as strawberries in spring, "how about if I call you back, oh in say, ten minutes, after I'm awake."

"What? You think I have ten minutes to wait for your sorry self? Get up and pay attention. I have a job for you. I expect you to accomplish it with the grace and aplomb you reserve for your finest deceptions."

Parson was struggling with his anger, as he often did when talking to his overbearing, arrogant boss. In fact, his anger was surging with such force through his body, he doubted whether he would need a cup of coffee this morning, or any morning ever again. "Okay, Hereford. This time, just remember," he continued with thinly-veiled hostility, "just remember that when I signed on to play bridge with you, it didn't mean working at nine o'clock in the morning. I don't keep those hours."

"Yes, I know. That is precisely why *you* work for *me* and *I* don't work for *you*. Speaking of your contract, you worthless bum, it's up for renewal." Hereford was enjoying the development of this conversation immensely.

Parson refused to be rattled by this. "I know my contract's up. We've done pretty well this year, Hereford. We won the Goldman Pairs and had two other regional pair wins. We won four knockouts and were in the finals of three others. We added two new conventions, which I was able to teach you in my usual simple style, so that you could play them the proper way. Our slam bidding, Hereford, has probably been better than almost every other client-pro pair in the country. And, I suppose you forgot, I have won enough masterpoints for you that you made the top 500 list again. All in all, pretty good in my book." Parson was holding his ground.

"So let me get this straight. You think that record is *good*. Good for who?" Hereford was not going to give an inch. This was, after all, part of the negotiation. "Good for a client," Parson threw back. Hereford was silenced by this truth, but only for a moment.

"Let's face it, Parson. You are, and always have been, overrated as a player. I don't think you deserve to get paid anything. Moreover, *you* should be paying *me*. I have salvaged your horrible reputation. My name and status have made you respectable again. You know this to be true." Hereford took the high ground again. Let not the truth stand in the way of a good negotiation. Hereford was beginning to warm to the idea of himself as Savior of the Damned, plucking people up out of ruin and making them something. He had made Parson. Well, almost.

"Okay, Hereford," Parson continued diligently. His concentration was fading quickly. His anger having temporarily subsided, he really longed for a cup of coffee, light and sweet. "You don't want to give me the bare minimum of a cost of living raise this year. I understand. You want me to starve to death or beg you for more money. Every year it's the same song and dance. Every year for the last five years we have the same discussion. Well forget it this year. I'm not begging—"

"—not begging or starving, either, with that fish-belly gut . . ."

"I don't care if I play with you or not," Parson persevered. "Do you think I can't get hired? Every year I get calls from clients wanting to hire me. Nice clients.

Respectful clients. Clients who don't call me at day-break. Don't ever call me this early again, Hereford. I'm a bridge pro, not a farmer. I have as many national titles as you have oil wells. I have earned the right to get up when I damn well please, and that time is noon." Parson had been on a roll. He had taken control of the high ground. He was just about to demand a fifteen percent pay increase and slam down the phone when he was startled by the softness of the voice on the other end of the line.

"Uh, Parson?" Hereford's voice was transformed, soft, respectful, almost tentative. "Parson, I understand how you feel about this."

"Yes," Parson said, triumphant, "I thought you might see it my way."

"In actuality, I called this morning to make you a deal for the next year. I don't really want to fire you, you know. I thoroughly enjoy playing with you," Hereford smiled into the phone. He had seen the light.

Parson was dragging the phone behind him into the kitchen to make coffee. He had yet to get a cordless phone; it seemed to be a waste of money. He hated wasting money. In any case, his phone cord stretched to reach virtually every corner of his small apartment. But, with his new contract, he might just spring for the new phone. He had seen one at Radio Shack that had 900 megahertz and 10 channels, and it was a matte black color. There was an answering machine that went with it; one that was digital so that the caller didn't have to wait for an hour to leave a message while the tape rewound. Perfect.

"So here's the deal I was thinking. You know that really prestigous pair event that is played at the Fall Nationals?"

"The Blue Ribbon Pairs?" Parson had happily put in enough grounds for exactly two cups of coffee. Waste not, want not, his mother always said.

"Yes, that's the one. Here's the deal. We win the Blue Ribbon Pairs this year and you get to keep working for me at your regular salary. We lose, and not only do you get fired, but I tell the entire bridge community how you got the nickname of 'Parson' in the first place. Just think about the headlines on the cover of *Bridge Digest*: 'Bridge Pro Impersonates Clergyman to Win Titles.' You see, Parson, I've done my homework. I happen to know that your reputation as a bridge player was nonexistent until you won the Barry Crane Top 500 two years consecutively. I also know that you couldn't get hired by anyone, you couldn't play on a good team. You couldn't get a good partner. Basically, Parson, your bridge aspirations were dead. My sources tell me that while you were visiting the National Bridge League headquarters in Memphis, you dressed as a minister, finagled your way into the main computer room, and got into the computer. You changed your year-to-date masterpoint total, winning one of the highest personal bridge honors in the country: the most masterpoints earned in one year. I know you did it twice. As I see it, if that bit of information comes to light, you will never work or play bridge again. I'll call you later in the week and we'll work out a plot to win the Blue Ribbon Pairs. For a man of your obvious expertise in deception, this should be mere child's play. Come hell or high water I'm going to win the country's most prestigous pair event. And," Hereford said, pausing dramatically, "so are you."

Hereford hung up the phone gloriously and smiled at himself in the mirror. He had seen the light. It was reflecting off the blade of his steel knife, just before he plunged it into the heart of his bridge partner.

* * * * * * * * * *

"Come hell or high water I will have Ford Maddox as my partner, Penny. Your job is simply to get him," said Vanessa the Contessa, her poodle-like presence permeating her bridge club. She pranced and yapped out orders in between skinny cigarettes, pausing occasionally to adjust the strap of her white patent leather spike-heeled sandals. To do this, though, was something of an event. It required not only cavalierly flinging her white mink stole (a sheer necessity in the Miami summers), back over her shoulder, but also tipping her body upside-down to reach the shoe area. This was indeed a reckless business, as the plastic surgeon who did her body work had followed her directions exactly, and she now had rather large, stupendous breasts that could easily cause a fatal inversion if her lovely blonde head traveled too much below her waist. Adjusted, she looked at Penny, her new club manager and director. "Well, did you hear me or are you ignoring me?"

Penny wanted desperately to tell the truth, but settled for diplomacy. "Vanessa, I hate to keep harping on the same point here, but I'm new in town and I don't know him."

"But yet you say he won't do it. If you don't know him, how do you know he won't do it?" Vanessa hated the thought of not getting her way.

"I didn't say he *definitely* would not do it; I said he most likely wouldn't do it. He is a very famous, high-ranking player. Pros like that play on high-profile teams with well established clients who have been playing bridge a long time. Pros like that charge lots and lots of money. Handfuls. Because they get results, they have reputations that they are not going to risk. I can't just go talk to him."

"Penny, look," Vanessa said in an attempt to be soothing that ended up merely patronizing. "First of all, Ford Maddox will want to play with me. I *have* handfuls of money. I *am* high-profile. You will offer him whatever it takes to get him to play with me. Secondly, dear, as to the problem of getting his number: just call up that director friend of yours who works across town. He knows Mr. Maddox. Quite well, in fact. When I used to play at that club, before I got totally disgusted and had to open my own, I saw them together on several occasions having a very good time. I always thought if Richard spent half as much time managing his club as he did having a good time, he would have a better place. In any case, Richard told me that they had been friends for years and years. That's when I decided I wanted to play bridge with Ford Maddox. So call Richard and have him put you in touch."

"Vanessa," Penny was trying hard to contain her irritation, "I guess you forgot one thing. *Richie* is going out of business because of you." She emphasized his name because she knew he hated the name Richard. She could picture him jumping every time this woman barked "Rich-ard" at the club. "I doubt I'll be able to get him to do anything for you," she added.

"Have you spoken with him since you've been in town?"

"Umm, yes," Penny wavered. She did not want Vanessa to know she had gone to Richie for a job first. And McDonald's second.

"Well, did you tell him you were working for me?" Vanessa felt like she had to drag this information out of Penny.

"No, uh, I don't think so, why?"

"It's simple then," Vanessa wondered how anything would run without her to oversee. "Call him up and ask him as a favor for yourself."

"Wait a minute, Vanessa, that's lying! I can't—no I won't do that to a friend of mine. That's really underhanded."

"Your job, my sweet, is to get Ford Maddox. Whom you have to call and what you have to say is not even remotely my problem. May I remind you of your paycheck and your bills. My advice to you is, do it quickly, get it over with, and move on with your life. Business is business."

Vanessa had teetered over to the coffee machine and was feigning ignorance of how it worked. This act had no impact on Penny; she had, only two days ago, walked in on Vanessa operating the machine with perfect proficiency. Penny now watched Vanessa's helpless woman routine with mounting disgust. This woman was anything but helpless. "Penny?" Vanessa crowed sweetly, "you know how to work this coffee machine, don't you dear?" "No, I don't," Penny lied, surprised at how easy it was. "I don't drink coffee." As Penny stalked out of the room to her miserable destiny of telephone calls, she carried with her the small satisfaction that Vanessa the Contessa would have to make her own coffee today.

* * * * * * * * * *

It seemed to Richie that he was experiencing a perverse kind of torture. His phone, equipped with a state-of-the-art broken answering machine, had been ringing ceaselessly, probably, in Richie's best estimation, since the dawn of time. Not only had the ringing telephone jolted him out of sleep, followed him into the ordinarily soothing morning shower, and persisted in ringing over the soft gurgling sounds of his coffee percolating, it stubbornly continued to ring right through the cacophonous racket his brain was making in its attempt to solve his financial problems. These problems were, ironically, why the phone was ringing in the first place. That this torture had been designed with him in mind, Richie was convinced.

It was fifteen days into the month, all his bills were late, and a good many of them would not be paid at all. Unfortunately, all of his best and second best excuses, as well as those totally unbelievable, had been used in the previous months, some of them twice. This meant that he really could not, under any circumstances, answer the phone. Here was the torturous part: that meant that Richie was missing phone calls from his friends, and for a fun-loving, easy going, people-loving person, that was cruel.

The situation, as Richie saw it, was bordering on bleak. If he didn't pay the alimony, he went directly to jail. (He had tried that once and even used one of his very best excuses on the judge, who evidently had heard all excuses, and Richie's didn't rate well. After three-hots-and-a-cot, Richie concluded the alimony must be paid.) If he didn't pay his rent, he went directly to the street. If he protested, he would probably have to face that same judge, who he was convinced didn't like him.

As if this weren't enough to contend with this month, Richie, in trying to make up the rent, made an unfortunate bet on *Two Wins Today* in the third race. The nag had finished second by a nose. Richie added up the numbers and realized the dearth of his luck: he had not only lost, but he had crapped out. Since he knew he'd rather face a grouchy judge than a grouchy bookie, he grudgingly forked over the money and that about did it for the rent.

Then there was the bridge club. Richie knew in his heart that this was the root of the problem; he could tell by the nausea in his stomach and the accompanying small, stuttering hiccoughs. Together, the duo signified "roots of problems," and they never failed him. It had all started to go south when that horrible woman had opened up Trumps. Richie had, until the dreadful moment of the Contessa's arrival, enjoyed the leisurely position of being, quite literally, the only game in town. His patrons loved him; it was as though he could do no wrong. He never worried about the condition of the club, the yellowing wallpaper, the darkening grout between the tiles in the dated bathrooms, or the chair pads beaten thin from the hours of weighty consideration spent on them. To him, this was homey, comfortable, familiar.

It had never occurred to him that others would not feel the same reverence and loyalty to the tradition of "Aces," Richie's club, that his loyal patrons would be swayed by the glimmer and glitz offered in the new club. But a steady stream of reports came back, and, like an ebbing tide, his clientele waned. At first it was whispered about in low tones, the conversation abruptly stopping if Richie were close. Then, like an oncoming storm, the descriptions of the splendor of the new club rained on all ears. Richie was drawn into the fervor, and his curiosity got the best of him. "What's it like?" he would find himself asking over and over again. He received detailed descriptions of the beautifully subtle wallpaper design that picked up the soft periwinkle blue in the plush carpet, the thickly padded chairs that had rollers on the bottom to make the journey from the new bidding boxes to the small side tables provided for your food ever so pleasant. The powder rooms (they had always been bathrooms at Richie's) were always stocked with a fresh supply of fragrant flowers and elegant little disposable hand towels that, again, matched the wallpaper. The sinks were somehow spotless all the time, feats that had Richie marvelling at the Herculean accomplishments of his adversary. The kitchen had a new coffee machine, readystocked with flavored coffees or cappuccino. No more taking a vote to see who would go next door to the Quick Shop for the decaf; this, too, was standard fare at Trumps. Above the microwave hung a new 17-inch color television. The set was always on, monitoring the news, a favorite soap, or a Saturday afternoon ballgame, just so the patrons could stay in touch with their world.

Richie, thinking hard, shifted in his seat. There was no way he could renovate; he simply didn't have the money to put back into the club. He needed a big loan, and he doubted whether the bank would loan him a quarter to call his mother. His arch enemy, Vanessa, somehow seemed to have cornered the bridge market. Not only did she have the clients, but all of the local pros had started to flock to her club. Some of them had taken to giving lectures and holding classes, bringing in even more people. It was a momentum thing, Richie analyzed. All he needed was something to shift the momentum. He felt a thought hovering at the back of his brain . . . slowly . . . it was coming . . . . Like an insistent child, the ringing phone demanded attention. Richie could not take it anymore. He clambered to pick it up, knocking over his coffee cup in the process. With hot coffee burning his leg, he answered the phone and attempted a foreign accent, "allo, can I 'elp you please?"

"Richie, is that you? What's wrong with your voice? You sound like a wounded cat." Penny had secretly hoped to get his answering machine, but, she was determined to do what she had to do.

"Hey Penny!" said Richie, forgetting his accent. Hearing her sweet voice on the other end of the line made him feel better instantly. He was very glad she had moved into town. "Were you able to find any work? What's the news? How are you, Penny?"

"Well, good and not so good," she replied honestly.

"Yeah, as you know I'm in that boat myself. A sinking ship, I like to call it."

"Things haven't gotten any better, huh?" Penny genuinely cared for Richie and guilt was now pumping through her veins.

"You know how it goes . . . but I'm not going to burden you with that. What's going on with you?"

"Listen, Rich, I'm in kind of an awkward position here—a bind, really."

Penny's heart was palpitating and she was beginning to sweat. She was faced with a monstrous dilemma; her job or her long-time chum. "I got a job—"

"Great, Pen. Great!" Richie beamed into the phone.

"And my new boss has said that she wants to hire a bridge pro." One-third of the job completed.

"No bind. I know lots of pros, Penny. I'll set you up." Richie's leg had stopped burning, and it was now very wet and getting cold.

"Well, Richie, actually, she wants Ford Maddox." Two-thirds done, she thought, oh boy.

"Ford, . . . hmm. He's hard to get unless you're playing at the top level. And he's expensive. How 'bout someone else?"

Richie heard talking out in the hallway. Sounded like it was at the bottom of the stairs. "No, it's gotta be Ford." Penny was definitely sweating now; she, too, was feeling cold and clammy all over.

"I can't see him doing it, Pen. He won't do it. But there are plenty of pros out there who are more than good enough for the job. Let's think."

But Richie was not thinking remotely about Ford Maddox or Penny or bridge pros. He was thinking that that voice he had heard was now walking up the stairs in the general direction of his apartment. He was thinking about excuses; he was thinking about the fire escape. He was thinking about pretending he wasn't home. He was thinking he should stop thinking and do something quick.

"No, it's really got to be Ford Maddox. I really need this, Richie. She said if I don't get Ford, I don't have a job. You're the only one I know who knows Ford well enough to persuade him."

Richie cleared his throat and lowered his voice, hoping Penny would not notice. "Who is this woman you're working for, Penny—she sounds like a tyrant."

Penny was audibly relieved. It would come out in the open. She would not lie to her friend, regardless of what happened. She would get another job. She would make it. "She *is* a tyrant. She's a horrible witch. To tell you the truth, Richie, I'm working for—" Just then there was a loud knocking, rather more of an angry banging, on Richie's door.

Richie, choking back the fear that had suddenly seized his throat, whispered out, "Call Ford—in the book—tell him I said so—gotta go."

The line went dead and Penny stood in the office of the bridge club for a moment, dazed. She should have felt relief. Instead, she felt like the black cloud that had been following her had suddenly started to sprinkle on her head.

Richie, realizing it was too late to escape, and aware he had no more excuses, went to the door. Pants stained and soaking wet from the crotch down, wearing no shirt, and perspiration dripping from his forehead, he did the only thing he could think to do. He swung the door open, looked the landlord in the eyes, and flung himself down on the floor, screaming, writhing, and foaming at the mouth, hoping in his last desperate moment to convince the landlord of his insanity or to scare him half out of his wits. At this point, Richie didn't care which it was.

* * * * * * * * * *

The famous Ford Maddox was feeling less than famous. He walked distractedly to the refrigerator, opened the door, saw a half-eaten B.L.T., a can of soda and a small piece of what he assumed was some very moldy cheese. Then, in a moment of clarity, he grabbed the soda, closed the door and decided he had to work out his problem. Once in a while, he told himself, hard times fall on everybody. Just have to work this out, that's all. Get a plan.

Ford flopped his athletic frame onto the couch and dialed the phone. Nobody better to call than his closest friend Meyer. Meyer was a genius at this stuff, he could always come up with a plan. Meyer had good solid horse-sense with a dose of cut-to-the-chase straightforwardness that Ford felt he could trust. In their green years, Meyer and Ford were a bridge partnership, "the M & M's" they were affectionately called. Then, as Life will have her merry way, Meyer got a job as an assistant to a private investigator and Ford had to make money any way he could, so he played bridge.

He played rubber bridge for ten cents a point until he had enough money to play in the higher-stakes game for a dollar a point. This meant that on a vulnerable grand slam hand he could win or lose more than two thousand dollars, and *that* meant that he had to become really good really fast or starve. He had also spent a lot of time playing at bridge clubs, getting paid $75 per session from his client partners. His main concern was eating, and following a close second to that was the task of building his reputation. This came, as most success does, excruciatingly slowly at first.

Ten years had passed, and after much hard work, he was able to stand alone in the penthouse of his career and smile at the soft glow of the more distant, dimmer lights of the bridge world. All that was not helping him now, he ruminated. Now, he was without a client and with bills to pay. He hoped Meyer would pick up the phone with a plan in hand and soon. As he thought this, he heard the richly resonating voice through the line, "Meyer here."

"Meyer," Ford wasted no time on the amenities with his friend. "I need a plan."

"You haven't found a new client?"

"Right, I need a client. And in lieu of that, I need a plan. I am without a plan. Planless."

"So let's backtrack for a moment. What happened to the last guy?"

"That was Ashenfelter. Jonathan B. He had a sudden inspiration to take a world tour with his wife this year. You know, the safari thing, the wall of China, all that."

"That would make playing bridge kind of a squeeze, so to speak."

"Yes, a helluva commute."

"Hmm. Okay." Meyer's mind shifted into its problem-solving mode. Ford, on the other end of the line, tried to stay quiet but drummed his fingers on the end table. "Are you tapping your fingers, Ford?" Meyer had the hearing of a mother.

"All right, I'll be quiet and let you think," Ford snapped. They had clearly had this particular exchange several thousand times during their friendship.

"Have you explored the possibility of playing as a sixth on one of the five-man pro-teams?"

"Yes. No go. There was one offer, but I can't stand the people on that team. Since I'm the newcomer, I'd get blamed for everything that went wrong during the matches. They could drop 10,000 IMPs at the other table, and somehow I would be responsible because I missed a reverse-double-end-play-super-squeeze-with-a-twist. The other pros would tell the client that any beginner could have made the play and hang me with the loss." As Ford spoke, he became more dejected. Today, he really hated his job. He should've been an accountant or the President or some other thing his mother really wanted.

"Yes, I know that's what happens." Although he knew his friend was struggling, Meyer did not compromise his practical approach. "That's the politics of professionalism. There'll be a fifth suit in the deck before most of those bridge pros put their ethics before their paychecks. But that's not our concern here. Let's consider all the options."

"Meyer, do you realize that the clients, these clients, who are successful enough to afford bridge pros, are somehow willing to believe everything their pro tells them. The clients obviously have enough intelligence to make a ton of money in the first place. What happens? They walk into a bridge club, or a national event, and their brain gets sucked out by aliens? They fall for the most base forms of flattery. They don't even check the scorecard, for Chrissake. The pro says, 'Joe Client, we just beat the best pair in the world by 100. But at the other table, the jokesters couldn't even follow suit. So we lost.' And the client believes the pro!" Ford was working himself up a good head of steam.

Meyer's logical mind continued to toss out options, "What about other teams? Have you called around?"

"All the other teams are full. There is nothing available for me."

"Have you called all the clients you know?"

"Meyer," Ford was exasperated, "I've been dialing for dollars for days now. That's what I'm telling you. I need a plan. There are no clients. There are only bills and more bills. Hold on a minute, please, my other phone line is ringing."

With that, Ford clicked over, glad to have a moment away from Meyer, who was, Ford thought, being especially obstinate about this problem.

"Ford Maddox?" a sweet voice asked.

"Yes, how can I help you?"

"Well, you can play bridge with my boss," Penny blurted out. Ford clicked back over to Meyer.

"Meyer, you're never going to believe this. This may be the answer to all my problems. Manna from Heaven. Let me call you back."

"Ask and ye shall receive," Meyer said, and hung up the phone. At this potential news he was greatly relieved, as he had yet to come up with a plan to satisfy Ford.

The phone only rang once before Meyer picked it up. "Okay, Meyer, this is the deal. A friend of Richie's just called me. Penny is her name—"

"Penny? Penny who?" Meyer exclaimed.

"Aaaahhm . . . McGill. Penny McGill." Ford had barely heard her last name over the sound of money falling from the heavens.

"Getoudda here! Penny McGill lives with me. That dirty dog."

It was Ford's turn to be shocked. "What?! You are living with someone? You were going to tell me, I guess, today?"

45

"No," Meyer laughed, "she's staying with me. She's been a friend of mine forever. We used to work together at the National Bridge League."

"So she's a friend of yours and Richie's and I've never met her. Why not? Do you all work for the C.I.A. and if I meet you all I'll be kidnapped and tortured by the Ruskies?"

"But wait," Meyer was still laughing, "Why did she call you?"

"That's what I've been trying to tell you. Your cover's blown. She wants me to play bridge with her boss. She got me a client." There was a heavy pause on the phone. "Meyer? Is something wrong?" Ford asked.

Meyer let out a long breath. Could be the beginning of a really big mess, imbroglio even. "Ford." Meyer didn't know where to start.

"Mey-er. Meyermeyer. What's the deal? Tell me please. You are not happy. I am very, very happy. This woman wants to pay me a boatload of money. Your friend Penny says that this client really wants to improve her game. She wants to win. She has been an ardent fan of mine for some time. I will be paying my bills and then some." Ford, phone in hand, was bouncing towards utter jubilation. Approaching glee. He had nearly started to skip around his living room, but restrained himself.

"Ford, I have heard some unpleasant things about this woman already, and Penny hasn't been working there very long."

"Everybody has idiosyncracies. The Anal-Retentive, the Obsessive-Compulsive, the Squeezing of the

Paste from the Center. My biggest idiosyncracy, until twenty minutes ago, was Absence of Funds. Lucky for me I didn't have to go through painful therapy. I'm cured."

"Ford," Meyer's voice was stern, "Have you met her?"

"No. I have not. Why?"

"Did you speak to her on the phone?"

"No. I did not. Would you like to tell me why you are impersonating a lawyer and interrogating me, Meyer?"

"Ford, in the off chance that Penny's stress is the result of some behavior of this client, some personality trait like Wackiness or some idiosyncracy like, say, Bitchiness, don't you think you should meet her and talk to her—just in case—before you take the job?" Meyer sensed danger ahead.

"Too late, Meyer the cynic and doomsayer. I'm already committed. I accepted the offer." Ford was weary now of all this analysis; he wanted to rejoice in his good fortune.

"Do not say, at any point, that I did not warn you, Ford Maddox. Mark my words. Big mistake."

"I'm glad you're right behind me," Ford laughed, his heart easy now. "I start on Monday at her club. I'm going to pay some of my bills and plan my own private celebration dinner, to which you are cordially invited, but your pessimism is not. Tonight, eight o'clock, Flannery's Steak House."

"You're finally going to pay your tab there?" Meyer parleyed. "This I gotta see."

Today was the first day Ford had ever looked forward to paying his bills.

One Club—I Pass

Like a vivid photo in the soft wash of memory, Vanessa's bridge club stood in the sweltering summer heat, coolly surrounded by palm trees. To the 1990's, it was defiantly Deco, painted in ice blues and greens. Ford wondered whether the inside could possibly live up to the promise of the snapshot exterior. Enchanted, he walked towards the entrance of the building. His eyes were blinded by the sun's glare glinting off the sign that bore the name "TRUMPS" in large bronze letters. A solitary gold Mercedes, the club's glittering sentinel, silently questioned Ford as he walked past. He crossed the cozy brick veranda and thought to himself that the white wrought-iron chairs dotting the brick floor looked, at best, uncomfortable. He wondered if anyone ever sat there. Probably not, he conjectured, not for longer than a short cigarette, anyway. He pulled open the frosted glass doors, walked through, and found himself in another decade. The interior reflected the Deco theme of the exterior; the rooms could double for a movie set of a 1920's Prohibition drama. The large rooms were stunningly historical. Authentic furnishings stood quietly in the dim light of the cold rooms.

As Ford looked around, he saw many bridge tables circled by comfortable-looking chairs, yet . . . strangely . . . he could not imagine playing bridge here. Maybe it was the room temperature: the coldness was paralyzing. It was far colder than any air conditioning Ford had experienced, and he had been in Miami a long time. The frigid air seemed to surround you in its stillness, draining the warmth from your body. Sleep was creeping across Ford's mind as he stood, cold and still, the latest piece of furniture to adorn the room. A shiver went up his spine and he shook open his eyes, surprised that they had closed. He quickly looked around to see if someone was there, but only the large, slow-turning steel fans that hung bluntly from the ceiling dared to punctuate the silent stillness of this frozen time. Ford softly stamped his feet and rubbed his hands together. Now fully awake, his thoughts darted briskly through his mind.

It was so cold, it reminded Ford of a book he had read in junior high. He thought the title was *Call of the Wild*. It was by Jack London, or Lou Jackson, or someone who had probably been to this club, in any event. It's the story of a guy who dies because he won't listen to common sense. All the characters in the book keep talking about how cold it is, warning the main character not to travel. Even the Huskie dog knows it is too cold to travel. The main character though, is hasty in his decisions and believes he knows the situation better than anyone else. So he ignores all the sage advice, embarks on his journey, and freezes to death. Ford was beginning to believe he might just be that character. This decision to play with someone he'd never met might have been a little hasty in the face of sage advice. As to death by freezing, he knew one session in this club would do it.

Suddenly, Ford heard the oppressive silence again, and worried that his regretful thoughts were too loud. But his mind would not stop rushing. What kind of a person would have this kind of a place? Was this atmosphere accidental, some thermostat under recall, or was it intentional? Ford heard the answer coming. Distant tapping: ticketty ticketty ticketty: little heels on cold foyer tile. The heels carried bird legs, and atop the spindles perched the ancient bird herself, fluffing and preening as she scrabbled down the hall. She was the only other living being in the place, leading Ford to conclude that this was Vanessa. As the bird-woman swooped into focus, Ford shuddered. He realized that waiting in this strange place had allowed him to prejudge this woman, and scolded himself soundly. But, he argued with himself, hadn't he learned early to trust his instincts about people?

In the salad days of his bridge career, the lesson had been etched into his memory. Then partners, he and Meyer were a couple of young, green hounds out to prove what a great system they played. If they roughed up one or two of the local club players in the process, it was all in a night's fun. They found themselves, one evening, off the beaten path and playing in a club game they had never been in before, or since. Round after round, they sat down at table after table, flashing an impressive convention card covered with ink and giving lots of explanations. Occasionally, one of the opponents was a little annoyed, but most people could tell that Ford and Meyer were genuinely sweet pups who intended no harm; they were just young and full of fire.

That came to an abrupt halt on the next to the last round, when they sat down against a couple of wily slimeballs dubbed, appropriately, Flim and Flam. Together, Flim and Flam were an intimidating force at a collective 600 pounds. They both had the look of experienced, expert players: confident, focused, unsmiling. They hardly looked up as the youngbloods sat down. Ford had a strange feeling in his stomach, but pressed forward with the cheerfulness of a spring day. The two men glanced at Ford and Meyer's sprawling convention card. Flim and Flam discussed a possible defense to a convention in tones so low only the carpet could hear them. A quiet fell on the table. Ford looked up at Meyer, who was studying his hand. Something was out of kilter, but Ford couldn't quite place it. And things with no name can be dangerous indeed.

The first board out, Ford ended up in six spades and had to guess the trumps. He had king-jack-ten-nine in his hand opposite the ace and three others in the dummy:

♣ A 8 5 2

♠ K J 10 9

Ford led the jack from his hand, and the guy on his left hesitated, sighed ever so slightly, and played low. Flim and Flam had mastered the ART OF THE HUDDLE: deliberate, deceptive, despicable. But Ford had read the performance like a book and interpreted this to mean that Flim did *not* have the queen, so he went up with the ace and successfully finessed the other way.

Convinced of the Flim-Flam sham, Ford was paying close attention when, on the second deal, he picked up:

♠ K J 8 4
♡ K J 6 2
◇ J 9 6
♣ A 4

Since he was playing five-card majors, he had to open the bidding with one diamond. Flim made a takeout double; Meyer passed. Flam furrowed the one long brow that scarred his sweaty pink face and started to think. His thoughts sweated, and he sweated thoughtfully. He sat, unaware of anything but his hand. This, it seemed, was a decision. But then so is whether or not to put milk in your coffee.

Turns out, Flam was looking at:

♠ 5
♡ 7
◇ A K Q 10 8 4 3 2
♣ 9 5 3

There was no question that Flam knew he was going to leave the double in and probably collect one of the biggest numbers in history, especially for defending against a one-level contract. But, he figured that if he left it in quickly, his opponents would know he really had them. That might cause Ford to run to a better place. On the other hand, if Flam sat there for several minutes and looked tortured, Ford would probably think that it was a marginal leave-in at best, and he might be tempted to stick it out in one diamond doubled.

Flam, in a moment of great reluctance, passed. Ford, though, was equally enlightened as to the theater that was going on around him. He thought to himself, *there's no way I'm staying in one diamond doubled; I don't care if this guy sits and stews till the next millennium.* Ford was confident. Redouble for takeout. The bidding ended with Flim and Flam playing in a routine three notrump, making five. Flam realized that having given a second-rate performance, he was in for only an average board. He snorted in disgust. The young sleuth Ford, foiling the deception, turned to Flam with a smile as wide as the Mississippi River was long. Gotcha, his dancing eyes glittered.

Ford, reminded of his keen table feel, focused again on the woman, and shuddered.

Vanessa was as small as a robin, as tough as a jay, and as old as a Phoenix. She approached Ford with the confidence of a hawk. Her rapacious eyes seized Ford, devouring every detail of his appearance. From his thick ebony hair, to his smooth face, to his strong hands, her eyes feasted on his athletic ease and stature. Alone but for her hunger, she greeted Ford with a smile that shivered in a thin veil of hospitality. "Mr. Maddox? I certainly hope you're Ford Maddox," Vanessa leered. Ford looked away, embarrassed.

"I am he, Ms. Vanessa. In cold blood." Ford attempted all of his boyish charm, not at all sure if he had succeeded. He was quite sure, however, that he had never had to reach so deep to find it.

"Oh," Vanessa replied with a head-toss and an exaggerated laugh. "All this," she said, surveying his entire 6'2 frame, as she gazed admiringly into his cerulean eyes, "and a sense of humor too. I am the world's luckiest woman."

Previously suffering from frostbite, Ford's quest for warmth was answered with a long, sickening, hot flash of realization. His role in this drama was becoming altogether too clear. His leading lady had a penchant for men significantly (more accurately, generationally) her junior, and she had written him into the part. Embarrassed, Ford shifted and nervously rested his hand on a nearby chair for support. *I just want a job*, he thought remorsefully. God, what a mess. He had to quell the torrid waters that were crashing on the beach of his small island of professionalism. Diplomacy on demand. Not really his strongest suit.

"Well," he said, meeting her eyes with a casual smile, "we are going to need it. Your assistant said you were an advanced intermediate who wants to become a great bridge player. That takes hard work, a good teacher, and a fair amount of luck." He had tried to be light and friendly, but he felt the whole thing went over like pork chops at a Bar Mitzvah.

Chafing at the rejection, Vanessa recoiled like a proud feline offered distasteful food. She stood poised for an angry attack. But, she calculated, this was neither the time nor the place if she wanted to possess this quarry. She sent her anger away, slinking back to brood in the dark recesses of her heart. "Ford, *may* I call you Ford—?" Her eyes narrowed ever so slightly.

"Please do," he interrupted her softly, trying to stop the swell of hostility. Vanessa would not be appeased.

"Ahem," she smiled demurely and batted her eyes, "please don't interrupt me when I'm speaking."

Oh boy, what a day already, Ford thought. This woman is actually annoyed that I am here to play bridge. Terrific. Should make things really easy. He smiled pleasantly, and said nothing. Vanessa continued in high tones, "I'm glad you're punctual. We have some time before the afternoon game starts. Let me show you around my club." She whirled on the points of her heels, a maneuver that must have taken years of practice. Ford wondered if, in the beginning, she had ever incurred any injuries doing that. There would be the obvious falling down and breaking of bones, but you could probably get a less obvious injury too. Pulling of the groin or hamstring, say. Hyperextension of the knee. Hell, if nothing else, you could get really dizzy from whirling that fast.

Immediately she began the club-tour monologue. This was the first clue that she had made a profession of showing her club. The gestures, laughs and jokes were impeccably timed, giving the seamless illusion of a warm, affable host. For Vanessa to appear warm was undoubtedly the crowning glory of her acting career, that much was clear. Months it must have taken her, Ford speculated. Years maybe. The tour was replete with pauses, giving the visitor ample opportunity to admire. He knew the drill. He smiled, nodded, and complimented her great taste and tremendous sense of style and history. Unbelievable, especially for a bridge club. An honor to play there (this one he thought was a little much, but she didn't even blink). Ford thought the only oversight was the absence of air sickness bags and ear muffs; he was badly in need of both. But, he was a professional, and by the end of the tour, he had soothed her ruffled feathers.

People began to arrive for the afternoon game. They fortified themselves with fresh orange juice, coffee, and delicious home-baked cookies. Vanessa and Ford had ended up in her office, watching the activity through a large window in the wall. Ford looked up to see the flash of a woman shooting through the crowd like a missile, heading directly for the office. The door opened, and before the woman could catch her breath, Vanessa started the introductions.

"Penny, this is Ford Maddox, our latest acqui—, er, the latest addition to our group," she oozed.

Penny set her bag down on the desk and put out her hand. "It's really terrific to meet you. I follow you in the magazines," she smiled genuinely. *A warm heart*, thought Ford. Must be tough in this place.

"It's nice to meet you too, finally. I just found out we have a couple of mutual friends."

Penny laughed. "Yes, I think we do. Let's talk later," Penny said, turning to her business. "I'm the director and I'm running a little late."

"As usual," Vanessa sniped. "Shall we go meet the patrons, Ford?"

Meet the patrons? Ford looked confused. "I'm sorry, Vanessa, what was that?"

"Well, darling, it's free press for you. It helps to get your name in circulation. It's an appearance."

"Vanessa, I appreciate that, although at this point in my career it's not much of a priority. We really need to spend some time going over the convention card and which methods we are going to use."

After the earlier misunderstanding, Vanessa could no longer contain herself. Her thousands of dollars in plastic surgery could not soften the ugly anger that overtook her face. In her very short tenure, Penny had learned this face, and she braced for the storm.

"I thought," she said, sarcasm dripping, "I thought that we could *communicate*. I play by feel, and usually, with a good partner, we have a sense of each other. I don't think we need to spend a lot of time discussing all that. If you play bridge with me, you will get to know me, and then you'll know, by inference, how I bid and play."

Ford had heard this line of reasoning before, and ignored it. "What about basic things like Stayman and Blackwood?" Ford asked.

"Well, of course I play those; everyone plays Stayman and Blackwood," she answered brusquely.

Of course, because everyone uses some kind of conventions, Ford thought to himself. He tried to press further, "What about negative doubles and transfers? What kind of raises do we play—limit, strong, weak? Do we do anything over their notrump?" Ford hoped that this list of questions might force her to realize the necessity for the discussion, or at least get some information so they could play.

Vanessa growled, "I said no discussion. That's enough. I'm a natural bidder. You are an expert. For the exorbitant fee I'm paying you, you will undoubtedly be able to figure out what is in my hand." She glared at Ford, challenging.

Ford, no slouch when it came to challenges, calmly replied, "In my career, I've found that no matter how close you are with your partner and no matter how well you communicate away from the table, there's no substitute for clarity about methods. It's difficult to second-guess a negative double, a weak-two bid or a transfer. To me, it's a lot easier if we talk about it up front." *Unless, of course, I am Creskin and you lend me your crystal ball,* Ford added to himself, tired of her silliness.

The people continued to mill about waiting to play. Out of the corner of his attention, Ford noticed that an impromptu fashion show had started just on the other side of the office window. He could hear the muffled ooohs and aaahs of the women admiring one another's outfits, and the occassional deep laugh of a man's voice. He deeply wished to be out of the office; he was beginning to feel claustrophobic. Penny, his only ally, had somehow slipped out and was nowhere to be seen.

"Well, Ford my sweet," Vanessa had bridled her anger, saddled it too, and was, in fact, preparing to break her new bronco. "I'm not paying you handfuls of money to have an easy time. I am paying you to play bridge. I am paying you to meet my needs."

Meyer's haunting words echoed through his mind, "What if she's a wacko, or worse yet, a grade-A bitch?" Eternity happens in moments, and Ford was having a moment. His heart flooded with regret and his mind flooded with thoughts. Mostly, Ford regretted the thought that "Meyer is always right." It was a thought he had often had.

Ford chose his words carefully. Practicality pays bills, but self-respect allows you to sleep at night. During the course of his career, Ford Maddox had played bridge with some kind players, an occassional brilliant player, a couple of beautiful players, one funny player, and a whole slew of rich players. He was impressed by nothing except a good heart, and as a result, he feared no one. He strongly believed he would always have enough, which gave him a great deal of freedom in dealing with people. Ford had developed a theory about money and people. Money makes you more of who you are. If you are a kind and generous person, you become more generous. If you are miserly and fearful, you become a grinch. And the power hungry people, well . . . history writes itself. With the tyrannical clients, and Vanessa was shaping up to be one of those, Ford tried to explain the concept of team. The problem was that tyrants, inherently, lacked the team-player gene. To a tyrant, teams were things you owned, managed and disciplined, but never played *on*. Observing Vanessa so far, Ford had categorized her as the tyrant type, to be dealt with as such. The cardinal rule of managing a tyrant was to show no weakness. Not a whipping boy today, thank you very much.

He took a breath, looked Vanessa directly in the eyes and said, "You are paying so much money because you have hired one of the best professional bridge players in the country. I am one of the best because I get results. I get results because I work closely with my clients and we have extended discussions about bridge. We work hard, we develop a solid partnership, and we win. We use convention cards because we use conventions. Let's go meet your friends and we'll discuss the conventions as they come up. We can fill out a card between rounds. How's that?"

Vanessa was a woman who was rarely at a loss. This turn of play, however, had left her uncertain as how best to proceed. She definitely wanted to maintain control of the famous, debonair Mr. Maddox; she did not want him to get away with this childish rebellion. On the other hand, she sensed somewhere in her stomach that perhaps he wasn't bluffing. He might not be afraid of her. She paused and considered, then decided to humor him for the moment. She would possess his spirit in the end; it was simply a matter of time and training. "Okay, Mr. Maddox. We'll do it your way this time. But I don't appreciate the tone in your voice at all. You *do* work for me." Vanessa twirled and swung through the office door, pausing on the other side for her escort.

Ford, with Vanessa unnaturally near his side, slowly made his way through the mass of people. He shook hands and smiled, accepted congratulations on his last tournament, all the while thinking of his salary, his bills, and what his life had come to. Ford had just avoided stepping into a puddle of self-pity, when in walked his nemesis, Hereford Willis III.

Hereford was a man who traveled en masse, flanking himself with an entourage whenever possible. Hereford had his favorites among his ever-changing coterie, though his favor was based on utility, not companionship. Utility is not always easy to decipher, and it would be easy to assume from a fleeting glimpse, that the extent of Parson's usefulness was bridge knowledge. Not so. For, despite the frequency and flagrance of Hereford's dubious actions at the bridge table, his bridge reputation remained relatively clean. This phenomenon was entirely due to the presence of Parson. Parson, having a much longer track record of questionable incidents, combined with the title of professional, drew all the attention of slanderous sharpshooters interested in trying to keep bridge a good, clean sport, or at least keep it free from cheating. Thus, Parson's utility was that of a decoy, attracting all spurious comment away from Hereford, like insects to fertilizer.

When Vanessa saw Hereford, she whirled on the back of one heel and became immediately effusive with all of those "You look so wells," "How've you beens," "Very happy you made its," and all the rest. This bland greeting act concluded, Hereford turned to Ford and said, "This is certainly unexpected, Ford, to see you here at a nothing club in nowhere Florida playing with a nameless client. The famous Ford Maddox, reduced to this. I predicted that the Ashenfelter gig was too good for you, Ford. Wouldn't last. Couldn't. Nope, this is where you belong. No bridge pro is worth what you get paid. See you at the table, there, son." Hereford just loved it when his little plans caused his enemies to suffer. He gallantly trotted off, leaving Ford yawning at the familiarity of it all. He shivered for the hundredth time today, and longed for a sweater to stave off the brutal cold of the bridge club.

Vanessa's face froze. She had never been more humiliated, nor more angry in her entire life. She turned to Ford and said, "Aren't you going to defend yourself? Why are you cowering like a beaten dog? Say something!"

"What is there to say, Vanessa?"

"Well how about that you've won more titles than he could ever hope to, especially with that slimy fishball he employs?" she prompted, stomping her bird foot.

"He knows that," Ford replied, unmoved.

"How about that this is not a nothing club in nowhere, and I'm not nameless! He knows my name, and he's a regular at my club. He just finished complimenting me again on my club!" Vanessa screeched at the indignity of it all.

"Vanessa, listen to me," Ford said calmly, "he's trying to get under your skin. He's using gamesmanship to try to get you to doubt yourself, your ability, and me. Don't let him win before we get to the table. Come on. Let's go sit down." *That annoying bastard*, Ford thought. *I wonder if he's going to succeed in ruining another day of mine.*

Vanessa assumed her perch at the prestigious Table One, South seat. Hereford and Parson were quick to slide into Table One's East-West seats. The end of the first round had left Hereford chuckling, Vanessa caterwauling, and Ford holding his head in dismay with Parson trying to console him. *Good God*, he thought miserably, *this day will never end. And when it does, there are 364 more to come. Maybe I should bartend.*

* * * * * * * * * *

The sound of hearty congratulations came from several tables away. "Well played, Maura!" Priscilla radiated with the glow known only to bridge players who grossly overbid, and then watch their partners declare as if they could see through the cards. After overbidding her hand by about two aces, she had tenuously tabled her dummy. Then, as Maura played card after golden card, Priscilla's remorse was erased and replaced first by redemption and finally—triumph. "Six spades doubled, making six. It's an absolute top." In a noble mood, Priscilla politely waited for the score to be entered, and then for the crushed opponents to move to the next table before turning again toward Maura and gushing, "I think we really ought to consider playing in Chicago."

Pensively, Maura began her response. "You know, I wouldn't mind playing in the Fall Nationals. So long as we don't play every day. There's a fantastic surgeon in Chicago I'd like to consult. I could see him on a day we don't play. He's just developed a colo-esophagal bypass which interests me."

Jarringly brought back to earth, Prissy thought to herself, *For Heaven's sake, Maura, why don't you just bypass your whole body and pour your food directly into the john?* Containing her silent frustrations, she said aloud, "Then it's settled. I'll make all the arrangements."

The rest of the game was uneventful, except that by 4:30 p.m., Prissy had airline tickets and hotel reservations for two. She couldn't wait to play, to be seen, to mingle with the great stars which the Nationals attract.

She had *had*, of course, the presence of mind to make sure there would be an in-flight movie—any movie. Watching grass grow for two hours would be better than listening to the further adventures of Maura's Wayward Organs.

* * * * * * * * * *

Stumbling through his front door, Ford didn't know if he was more hungry, tired or frustrated. His adrenaline had been pumping all day and the back of his shirt was still soaking wet. Nothing worse than being wet and cold all day. He was trying to decide if it was better to be clean or full when he heard the phone ring. It was Meyer asking about the day. "Well," Ford said dejectedly, "it was nothing short of an absolute nightmare—in color, with surround sound. One of those nightmares where you are screaming but no sound is coming out of your mouth; no one can hear you. And the bad guys just keep coming."

Meyer made some kind of brusque noise resembling, "Order a pizza, I'll bring the beer," and hung up.

Ford crawled out of his clothes and crept quietly into the shower. He felt thrashed and shredded. Spending the remainder of his life in bed under the covers seemed like a really attractive career path. How Parson did this, day in and day out, he would never know. As the healing hot water massaged the tension out of his body, his awareness spread like a flashlight in a dark room. He had to get out of this situation. He could, under no circumstances, continue working with Vanessa, the Angel of Death.

The two old friends did not greet each other. They understood each other in that quiet, unspoken way of men. As Meyer opened the beers, Ford put the cardboard pizza box on the kitchen table and grabbed the spicy red pepper from the cabinet. Hungry, they ate and drank for a while in silence; the pizza was piled high with artery-clogging toppings and the beer was deliciously cold. When the hunger had subsided, Meyer turned to Ford and asked earnestly, "So, when did you know you were in trouble?"

Ford snorted and shook his head, his mouth still full with pizza. "She's . . . ," he swallowed. "That place looks like a movie set out of the 1920's. Have you been there?" Ford didn't know where to start.

"No—," Meyer was about to go on, but Ford continued.

"She's got a strange thing going on. I think she used to be an actress, or she wants to be, or maybe she just is an actress. Everything is very dramatic with her. She is always 'on stage,' performing for whoever is around. Very dramatic. From the moment I met her. She hired me to meet her customers, I think."

"That's not too surprising. People like to be seen with famous people, and, in this field, you're famous. Incidentally, people are also very dramatic. Gives them a sense of purpose. It's not personal."

"Yeah. You go play with her. She can drag *you* into her purpose and parade *you* around her theater. Then, when you get tired of it, put on the black hat for the bad guy, and she'll shoot you. Then tell me it's not personal."

Meyer laughed and pushed himself back from the table. "What else?"

"Okay. So it's not bad enough that you walk into this club that looks a movie set for some Chicago mob flick. Everything's too perfect. Except that it's so cold in this joint that you know, secretly, they've got bodies hanging like beef in the back room. Not a soul in sight. Very weird. Up comes this woman who, no lie, looks just like a blonde bird with boobs out to here. Great, I guess, except that she's about a hundred years old trying to look like twenty-five. Why? Then she tells you she 'plays by feel,' whatever that is. Frankly, at that point, I figured she was going to whip out a crystal ball and tell me she was psychic. Or start sacrificing small animals—"

"Sounds like you were the sacrifice," Meyer chimed in, grinning.

"Exactly. Now you're with me. Did I tell you how cold this place was? People showed up wearing sweaters like it was a New York winter. So there you are getting your head handed to you because you, a bridge professional, want to discuss bridge methods with your client. She plays by feel."

"Yes, you mentioned that."

"Yeah. 'Okay,' I think to myself, 'She's a little nuts, but hey, who isn't. She's paying me. Besides, how much worse can it get, right? A year of wearing sweaters and guessing what your partner's holding. Big deal.'"

"Yep. Anyone can wear sweaters for a year. Wearing them in Florida, that's a little challenging, but it can be done. Sweaters pay the rent."

"Exactly. A new movie. Then," Ford paused for a little drama of his own, "then Hereford and Parson show up. At her club, to play bridge. And we all start at Table One, together."

"The tie that binds. Togetherness, a great thing."

"Swell. I start to get that sinking feeling, but I stop myself and say, 'Self, it's just a couple of boards. Hell, I can play with anybody, against anybody, for a couple of boards.' Or so I thought. Hereford decides to take this opportunity to make a public show of his very pronounced dislike of me. Parson, in an unprecedented show of spine, sympathizes with me. This is the point I realize, beyond a shadow of a doubt, that I am deep in enemy territory. Behind the lines. When Parson is on your side, you are on the wrong side. We take the cards out of the board for the first deal. Naturally, my partner, the fire-breathing dragon, has refused to discuss any conventions. Imagine her surprise at this deal:

Vul: None   FORD
Dlr: South   ♠ A J 4 3
                ♡ J 9
                ◊ Q J 8 5
                ♣ 8 6 5

HEREFORD   PARSON
♠ 9 8 7   ♠ 6 2
♡ 7 6   ♡ A 8 4 2
◊ 7 2   ◊ A 9 6 3
♣ K Q J 10 7 4   ♣ A 9 2
         VANESSA
         ♠ K Q 10 5
         ♡ K Q 10 5 3
         ◊ K 10 4
         ♣ 3

"Nobody was vulnerable. She opened the South hand with one heart and Hereford overcalled with a preemptive jump to three clubs. I made a negative double, of course, and Vanessa had an easy three-spade bid.

WEST	NORTH	EAST	SOUTH
HEREFORD	FORD	PARSON	VANESSA
—	—	—	1♡
3♣*	Double**	Pass	3♠?

* = Preemptive
** = Negative

"Should I raise this to four? I never got the chance. Vanessa calmly passed my double, treating it as penalty. Instead of reaching three or four spades, cold for ten tricks, we were in the ridiculous position of defending West's three clubs doubled. Who, and I want you to name names, would have thought that in this day and age a duplicate player would treat my double as penalty?"

Meyer could barely get the words out between laughing fits. "So what did you do?"

"Glad you are enjoying yourself."

"Laughter aids in the digestive process, and I ate a lot of pizza, so finish the story," Meyer laughed.

"So, anyway, I led a trump and continued trumps at every opportunity. Declarer could never ruff a spade in dummy, so we beat it a trick, but plus 100 was sure to be a bottom. Naturally, I ask her—nicely, too—'How high do you play negative doubles?' Her response, predictably, was 'Only on the one and two levels. You should have known that.' How? By Divine Enlightenment? Maybe we should use marked cards, I wanted to say, the Beginner's Aid to Telepathy at Bridge. Nonetheless, when she realizes that I don't have a penalty double, she is furious. The best part of the whole story is that all of her plastic surgery has left her skin stretched so tight over her facial bones that she can't even get really angry. She doesn't have the room. The eyes begin to bulge, the lips purse, the redness in the face and then—poof. Her face can't even contort and grimace. Hereford, the dirty dog, decides to see if he can push her over the edge. She's snapping her cards in a rage, we're definitely going to get a bottom, and he's sitting there all tan and relaxed, making my life miserable by laughing at her. Laughing without a care in the world. I have never smoked in my life, Meyer, but I wanted to right then."

Meyer, thoroughly enjoying the story, suggested they move into the living room and make some popcorn. Ford, rolling his eyes, agreed to the former. As Meyer settled into the weathered leather couch, Ford freshened the beers and continued his story.

"Since I value my life, I didn't think it was prudent to press for more discussion of our methods after the disaster on this first hand. How bad can it really get, I think to myself. The odds of this sort of thing happening again are remote at best. We'll talk about it after Hereford and Parson leave the table. So we pick up the cards for the second board.

"Not vulnerable against vulnerable opponents, I'm holding, as dealer:

♠ 8
♡ Q 10 8 7 6 4 3 2
♢ J
♣ 10 6 5

"What do you do? My partner, Satan's lovely Bride, almost popped a cheek implant on the last hand, so you surely don't open four hearts. Whether or not she's psychic, when it comes to clients and bridge, my money says Vanessa comes from the school where you need eight cards headed by the ace-king-queen-jack, hell maybe even the ten, for a four-level opening bid. I wasn't going to pass; I'd much rather preempt. So I settled for three hearts.

HEREFORD		PARSON
♠ K J 10 9		♠ A Q 7 6 5 2
♡ A J 5		♡ 9
◇ 7 4 3 2		◇ A Q 6
♣ K 8		♣ A 9 2

HEREFORD	(FORD)	PARSON
—	(3♡)	3♠
4♠*		6♠!
Pass		

* = Slow

"Parson overcalled with a prompt three spades. My partner the cannibal passed. Hereford, man of inimitable integrity that he is, took forever and a day to bid only four spades. The world was created in less time than it took him to bid. I'd love to see their bridge notes; I guess slowness means extras in their system. I think he was worth a four-heart cuebid, but why play honestly when it's just as easy to inform partner with your tempo. So hang on, it gets really good now. Parson bids six spades and Hereford chuckles to himself. Chuckles! At this point, my head is reeling. Never mind that it's virtually cheating to bid after a slow four-spade bid like that, but then to jump to slam?"

Meyer shook his head in slow disbelief. "Unbelievable," was all he could say.

"Meyer, these guys not only play at clubs, they play at tournaments. It amazes me they are allowed to play. Why don't they just bring two cell phones so they can discuss the hands as they bid?"

"It would be less obvious. Did you call the director?"

"To be honest with you, Meyer, I wasn't even going to get involved. Besides, Parson would just say 'How did I know Hereford's slow four spades was based on extra values? Maybe he was deciding between passing and raising—he might have had a bare minimum.' I can hear it now. They have a great thing going. This is one of the biggest problems with club play today. It is so common for players to huddle to get to the right contract, that when a pair like Parson and Hereford do it, there's no recourse."

"I don't know about that. This particular auction was pretty flagrant. I think there's a big difference."

"No, not really. To me, all this kind of stuff, tempo, huddling, sighing, all that is on the same continuum." Ford had had a really bad day. He was thoroughly annoyed, and wasn't about to give anyone any slack.

"Maybe . . . in a way." But, Meyer thought, it was excessive to indict the entire world. "Most people at the club level don't intend to be unethical. That's the difference. I know Parson fully intends to be unethical."

"There is no difference, or it's very small. 'Intention' is the intention to win, and everybody who does that crap, does it with the intention to win. We'll discuss it later, after you have the 8 x 10, full-color picture of the horror of my day. Anyway, the Barracuda, my lovely partner, led her singleton king of hearts and this was the full deal (ROTATED FOR CONVENIENCE):

73

Vul: N-S
Dlr: East

<pre>
                    HEREFORD
                    ♠ K J 10 9
                    ♡ A J 5
                    ◊ 7 4 3 2
                    ♣ K 8
VANESSA   FORD
♠ 4 3   ♠ 8
♡ K   ♡ Q 10 8 7 6 4 3 2
◊ K 10 9 8 5   ◊ J
♣ Q J 7 4 3   ♣ 10 6 5
                    PARSON
                    ♠ A Q 7 6 5 2
                    ♡ 9
                    ◊ A Q 6
                    ♣ A 9 2
</pre>

WEST	NORTH	EAST	SOUTH
VANESSA	HEREFORD	FORD	PARSON
—	—	3♡	3♠
Pass	4♠ (slow)	Pass	6♠!
All Pass			

"Parson's play was easy. He won the heart lead, and ruffed a heart high. He drew trumps and ruffed the last heart high. Then he played the top clubs and ruffed a club in dummy, leaving:

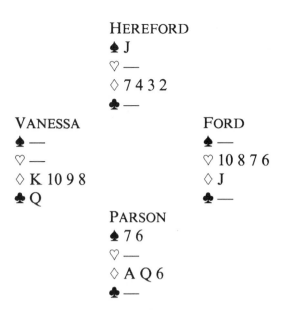

HEREFORD
♠ J
♡ —
♢ 7 4 3 2
♣ —

VANESSA
♠ —
♡ —
♢ K 10 9 8
♣ Q

FORD
♠ —
♡ 10 8 7 6
♢ J
♣ —

PARSON
♠ 7 6
♡ —
♢ A Q 6
♣ —

"The lead was on the board and he played a diamond. When my jack came up he knew what to do. From the play I was known to have eight hearts, three clubs, and one spade. He knew my jack of diamonds was a singleton, so he simply ducked it. I had to lead a heart and give him a ruff and sluff. He threw his diamond queen and ruffed in dummy and claimed 12 tricks. Parson courted death from yours truly when he started to gloat about how easy the hand was to make. I nearly had my hands 'round his lousy white neck, when we were all stunned by the unearthly sound from my partner's seat. I looked up just in time to see Vanessa's head spin around, and experience the fury of Hell's Dark Queen scorned by a Parson.

"The bloodcurdling invective that flew out of her beak was a ghastly reign of terror. We all cringed and tried, unsuccessfully, to disappear. Even Hereford blanched under that year-round tan of his, until, that is, it became evident that I was the object of her hatred. At this point, I knew it was shaping up to be a great day." Ford paused for a moment to take another bite of his now cold pizza slice. Story-telling was hard work.

Meyer impatiently prodded him. "What was she saying?"

"Hmm," Ford reflected, "it was like having aliens perform surgery on you in the mother ship. It was kind of traumatic. I don't remember much, just a voice screaming, over and over, 'Why didn't you throw your jack of diamonds on the second round of spades? I thought you were an expert!'"

"What good would that do?" Meyer shook his head.

"Exactly," Ford replied emphatically, "if I showed out on the diamond from dummy, Parson would simply stick in the six and endplay Vanessa. She'd have to give a ruff and sluff or play back a diamond. On second thought, I wish I *had* thrown the diamond jack just to see her suffer by getting endplayed. We probably all would have been treated to a display of her morphing into a large, winged creature with red eyes and fangs."

"Okay, as long as it's on a movie screen. Nothing live." Sage Meyer.

"Yeah, my life as a latenight B-horror flick. Seriously though, what am I going to do? I've gone from the proverbial frying pan right into the fire. And it's hot!"

Divine Wrong

Ford was in the middle of enjoying his morning. After eight hours of comatose sleep, he got up and checked his body for any visible lacerations from yesterday's battle with the creature from the black lagoon. There were none. And, memory being what it is, there was very little recollection of the pain of the nightmare. A couple of times during his morning run, his mind flashed on Vanessa's angry face, but it melted quickly in the bright sunlight. After a hearty breakfast, his mind was free, and he called Meyer, hoping the P.I. business was slow today so they could go play a quick nine holes.

Penny was also in the middle of her morning, though "enjoying" was hardly the word for what she was doing. "Suffering" was a more apt description of Penny's state of being. Stealing a look at her watch, she calculated it to be one hour and seventeen minutes that she had been cooped up with Vanessa. Vanessa, having no sense of time and apparently unlimited energy, had been ranting for the duration. That such a petite woman could endure the sheer velocity of the anger that propelled her was amazing; that she could maintain this pitch for over an hour was miraculous. Penny realized her sole function was to look attentive and nod periodically, giving the illusion of agreement.

Evidently, Miss Vanessa had had a less than stellar bridge game with her latest acquisition, Ford. Penny also gleaned, astute listener that she was, that Mr. Maddox was a complete and utter bumbling idiot given a deck of cards, and that it was an abomination, nay, highway robbery, that he was paid so much for his services. How he could have such a lack of sensitivity to Vanessa's bidding was astounding for a man of his alleged repute, and his lack of awareness on a simple hand involving a diamond jack led her, Vanessa, to question those who had reputed him in the first place. Penny, who was becoming increasingly desperate and sweaty, made several unsuccessful attempts to do her paperwork. Vanessa, the ever-present actress, was finely tuned to her audience and would simply raise her voice a couple of decibels if she sensed flagging attention. Finally, Penny could no longer choke back the bile that kept creeping up into her throat. She looked directly at Vanessa and said, "Well, if he's such a rotten player, then why don't you fire him?"

The plainness of the question startled Vanessa, and for a moment, Penny thought she had been too direct. But really, if you're that unhappy, change it. She hoped, slapped with the obvious, Vanessa would halt the attack. Unfortunately, though, Penny misgauged both the depth and type of Vanessa's anger. It was that sort of gushing anger that springs from an endless geyser deep in the soul and has nothing much to do with anybody in particular. The danger is that it can, and will, attach itself to anyone or anything standing within a football field of it, and Penny had just called attention to herself. Vanessa, tantalized by the possibility of blaming the blameless, turned her wrath toward Penny.

Brimming with haughty indignation, Miss Vanessa continued her scene: "My dear fool, to fire Mr. Maddox would be far too good a punishment for him. I would much rather make him suffer the consequences of his own insufferable ego. He mustn't disregard me in such a manner. Too busy to meet my patrons, is he? He has that crass air of pragmatism so clearly marked in people of his age. He will learn, though, life is more than practicality and considerations for the self."

For the love of God, Penny thought, *she's off her rocker. She's lost it this time.* Hesitating, Penny considered whether Vanessa was worth enlightening on this point. You are on the road to disappointment if you confuse a bridge pro who plays cards with a maître d' who meets, greets, and seats. There's just no way around it. It's a question of professionalism, not selfishness (and what happened yesterday, anyway?) This battle was definitely not worth it. Let Ford fight this one, Penny decided; I am neither a bridge pro nor a maître d'. Penny fixed her eyes on the empty wall and said nothing.

Vanessa's words fell flat in the quiet room. For Vanessa, the silence was indicting; she had to have a reply or face her own absurdity. "Don't you think, Penny?" she asked pointedly, eyes challenging Penny's silence.

It hadn't taken long for Penny to develop something of an aversion to Vanessa's sacrificial tendencies. Vanessa equated sacrifice with loyalty. Today, Ford was on the chopping block and Penny was being tested. Tomorrow, it could be the other way around. Penny thought all of this character assassination was a waste of time, simply avoiding the issue. By focusing on other people's badness, you relieved yourself of having to get to the real deal, the thing that was really bugging you. Determined not to be bullied by someone else's anger, Penny took a deep breath, and with courageous compassion said, "Vanessa, what is it exactly that's bothering you about this whole thing?"

Vanessa's face visibly softened, and there was a small opening of honesty. "I don't understand why the game of bridge has to be burdened with all of these conventions. I just want to play natural, pure bridge. I enjoy the game tremendously just as it is. Ford is just the opposite. He wants to complicate the game by using a lot of conventions and alertable bids. I fail to see the point. It's very frustrating."

Penny knitted her brow. A bridge pro wanting to play a lot of conventions with a client? Baffling. Usually the rule of thumb, in that case, was "less is better." She pursued, "what do you mean, Vanessa, what did he say?"

"Well," Vanessa said, a small pout scampering across her dry red lips, "he said he wanted to know if I played negative doubles or transfers."

Penny tucked a wayward strand of chestnut hair behind her ear and smiled. "He's just trying to go through the system with you," Penny reassured her. "Those are pretty general questions. Besides," Penny continued, warming to the subject, "even specific questions and conventions help you to get to the best possible contract. And the alerts, they're necessary. We can't have innocent new players coming to the game and not alert them if a diamond bid is artificial and shows hearts. There's nothing wrong with saying 'alert' to draw your opponents' attention to the fact that a bid is not what they might think it is."

"I'm not sure what you mean. It seems to me that all of these different approaches and methods and ways of bidding—all of it—get in the way. How many different ways can you say 'I have hearts?' I just don't see the need for any new conventions, alerts, or systems either. We have plenty of them as it is. Conventions are for salesmen and Elks. We can play straightforward bridge with what we have. Why allow any more?"

"Think about it, though," Penny softly reminded her, "what if people had said that fifty years ago, when Stayman and Blackwood were invented. They were a pain to learn, but now they're indispensable to bidding, right? Scientific methods allow you to do more than tell partner that you have hearts; you can tell her that you have two heart honors, no spades and diamond support."

"Yes. You have a point there." Vanessa was pensive. "But you have to agree that having to know all of these things just makes the whole game more difficult. It's not even enough to know what you play, you have to know every little thing your opponents play as well. It's terribly exasperating just trying to play a hand sometimes." Vanessa clicked her heel on the floor for added punctuation.

"Oh it drives me nuts, too, at times. It's very hard because when you first start playing bridge and you fall in love with it, no one ever tells you that the challenge keeps growing, that it's impossible to master the game. You get to be an intermediate, and you think to yourself, geez, I'm getting really good. Then you sit down against an expert pair and you realize how much further you have to go. The whole process can be very frustrating, no doubt about it. The point is, though, that the game challenges you on every hand to rise to the mental test: your concentration, your insight, your table feel."

"It's not that I mind the difficulty of the game," Vanessa replied quickly. "I just find it very annoying to sit down for a game of bridge at the club, and pick up some hoodlum's convention card that's completely covered with all sorts of notes. It's too much to process in thirty seconds. And then the bidding starts and goes 'one club, alert, one diamond, alert, skip bid, alert, please get me some coffee, alert.' I detest that. Alert! Why alert? What am I going to do about it? I don't even know what half of those things mean."

Penny could definitely sympathize with that. It is frustrating when you've been playing cards for years and a couple of college kids sit down who are better than you, and they want to be sure you know it. They chatter away, miserly squirrels who have stored all their information and are dragging it out now, just as you're trying to sort your cards and count your high-card points. Lots of them are nervy, and get really patronizing when they have to explain what *two-left-twists-after-an-odd-under-three-card-upside-down-flip* means for the second time to the old ladies, old being any woman over twenty-four. When will these kids realize that they would have to explain less if they explained better? Instead of giving the name of the bloody convention, the inverted minor pineapple, just say what it means: partner has six diamonds and the ten of spades. The urchins, drowning in their intellectual posturing, had evidently missed the point of active ethics.

On more than one occasion, Penny had had to restrain herself from doling out the discipline their mothers had unfortunately spared them. Many of these young, bright players needed to spend a little less time being condescending and a little more time remembering to respect their elders. One of Penny's favorite stories involved a wonderful Memphis woman who lost count of her age after 70, but kept her wickedly sharp intellect. This woman, Leta, was unabashedly admired by all as one of the most humble, gracious players in the South. Midway through the session at a local sectional, a couple of young men arrived at Leta's table. Their attitude and bluster did not phase Leta, who coolly sipped iced tea between rounds. The two whippersnappers flopped down East-West against Leta and her partner. They thrust their convention cards, all the masculinity they had at the time, onto the table with the announcement: "Eastern Scientific, upside-down carding, 10-12 notrumps."

The first pimply-faced lad opened with an artificial and forcing two clubs holding:

♠ 8
♡ 4
◇ Q J 10 8 7 5 4 3 2
♣ 9 5

This youthful pair ended up stealing the hand in five diamonds undoubled, down four, giving them a top score on the board; Leta's side had a laydown game available the other way. Hormones clamoring for recognition, the knaves gloated loudly at their opponents' fate. They ignored the old woman when she called the tournament director. Looking up at the director, Leta said mildly, "I have a problem with the two club-opening. Please consider what this gentleman," her kindness lingering around the word, "opened two clubs with."

The second scoundrel began wagging his tongue, "So what? He can open whatever he wants. We told these people what we play. It's not our fault they can't follow along."

The director was having none of it. "If that were the case, I wouldn't be here, would I?" Turning to Leta he asked, "Then what happened?"

"They ended up in five diamonds down four. However," she said patiently, "it's our hand."

"I see," the director said. His stern eyes held the boys as he addressed the table, "I'm awarding (N-S) an average plus and the opponents (E-W) an average minus, with a three matchpoint procedural penalty."

Jaws swinging like broken gates in the wind, the stunned boys stammered in protest. "What?!" the first one managed to get out. "You're favoring your old regulars. What kind of a ruling is that?"

The director replied evenly, "I guess you forgot that it's illegal to psyche a two-club opening. Not all of our players have such memory lapses." With that, he winked at Leta and walked away, leaving the two embarrassed neophytes struggling for their composure.

But Leta was kind-hearted and did not let them struggle too long. She smiled softly and said, "It's all right. We've all prejudged people before. It always costs

you, but this time you are really aware of how much."
With that, she picked up her cards and settled back into
her chair.

Penny rested her arms on her desk. The last twenty minutes had given Penny a greater understanding of
Vanessa's moodiness, her anger, her snippy quips. She
felt she had a deeper insight into Vanessa's character.
Graced with a big heart, Penny's compassion was still in
the running for the woman that others deemed a cold
frog. After all, Vanessa had bought a bridge club because she loved the game. And ironically, here she was
playing in her own club, with a pro she didn't understand, against people who intimidated her. *It would
probably make me kind of bitchy myself*, Penny thought
charitably. "Just think, Vanessa, after you've played
with Ford a while you'll be right in the swing of things,
alerting all over the place. By the time you're done playing with him, think how much you will have learned. A
great opportunity," Penny concluded enthusiastically.

This, evidently, was more vulnerability than Vanessa could bear. She whipped her head around and
snapped at Penny, "I don't give a damn about opportunity. In my life, I have made my own opportunity. If you
think you can sugarcoat this situation, you cannot. I
have not forgotten that you made an egregious error in
hiring Ford Maddox. I hold you fully culpable. I think
we both know that you are very lucky to still have a job,
considering what a debacle you've made of everything. A
very unpleasant mess for me to clean up."

Penny could not believe her ears. She was
stunned. Flabbergasted. Bordering on shocked. Shot

down in the flight of compassion, Penny had been fatally wounded. Vanessa swirled out of the office, the door closing heavily in her wake. *I will remember this*, Penny thought angrily. *When the time comes, I will remember.* It occurred to her that this was not the first time she had been hurt simply for trying to be kind and reasonable.

* * * * * * * * * *

Parson was in the middle of his dank apartment, with no knowledge at all that it was morning. He had been awake, or at least not sleeping, for most of the night. The blinds were shut tight, arresting any trace of sunlight daring enough to stroll by his window. He nervously scurried about in the gloom, sorting through the molehills of clothes that sprang up from the bedroom floor. He was searching for an idea. Hereford's demand that they win the country's most prestigous pair event, the Blue Ribbon Pairs, had rudely roused Parson from his complacent career as a purveyor of bridge peccadilloes. Parson was well aware that the American public would see affordable health care before he and Hereford could legitimately win that event. To perform this miracle, Parson needed a plan from the realm of the extraordinary, the superlative, better yet, the viable. The quest for such a plan had not only stolen his sleep, but just about every waking moment as well.

A normal person would crack under such pressure; however, Parson shared many characteristics with the organism that had dominated the evolutionary stronghold for eons: the cockroach. Above all, he was, like the cockroach, a survivor. Hard to control, harder still to kill. He moved with amazing rapidity, and had a hard, thick skin that repelled the most virulent insults. He darted deftly through night's darkest hours, a fearless guerilla soldier when the bounty was right.

Parson considered many schemes. Most of them could be pulled off, but not at the championship level: ironclad security. His mind returned several thousand times to the providential hour of his fortuitous blunder. Parson and his computer had spent many hours together in a united fight against Life's dreariness, and that particular Wednesday night, a few months ago, was no exception. Having been born with the havoc-wreaking rebellion gene prominently featured in his personality, he spent most of the computer time on the Internet prowling around looking for ways to stir the old pot. That night, he had found it. Through the forces of dumb luck, he had found himself an accidental tourist in the main computer system of the National Bridge League. He cherished any fantasy that cast him as David to an organizational Goliath, and so, for the baseless but frequent motive of ego, Parson set about wreaking havoc in the League's computer system. Eventually, long after perseverance had become tedium, he broke the access code for the deal generator.

Though protected like the Coca-Cola formula, once accessed, the League's computer program was unmistakably ordinary. It was used to generate deals for each tournament. After Parson accessed the program, he input one hand as a test. Coveting fame and recognition, in deed if not in name, he had turned fiction into fact with only a slight plagiarism, programming all 13 hearts to end up in the same hand. Parson thoroughly enjoyed the result. Everyone was talking about the hand, and the stir of speculation that surrounded it was satisfying, at least for the moment. Rumor was that the League was suspicious, but of course—and here Parson beamed proudly—there was no way to prove any foul play.

There had been only one minor trouble. Parson, not really expecting to find a way into the system, hadn't been keeping track of what he was doing. When he tried to retrace his steps, something froze his computer, and he became afraid that the League's computer was tracing his call. So he was left with a perfect scheme but no way to replicate it.

The torment of Hell is a very personalized thing. He was increasingly frustrated as he tossed his clothes into laundry baskets preparing for the journey into the basement. Winning the Blue Ribbon Pairs would be easy if he could input the deals in advance. How were those access codes derived? If he just knew that . . .

The phone jangled harshly in his ear. He scowled. He was not expecting any calls. Screw it. He was busy. The phone rang and rang. It kept ringing. The tension blossomed in his head, a beautiful flower opening to the sunshine. *This must be Mother*, he thought, regretfully; *she's the only one rude enough to let the phone ring forever.* If she didn't get through now, he knew that there'd be a lot of whining to deal with later, after she had had time to stew for a while. He's never around, she would say. What if something really terrible had happened and she needed to reach him? She doubted if he loved her at all, since he was never around, which was just fine, she thought, for a boy whom she burdened into life. "Okay, you old witch," he said out loud to no one, "I'm coming." And with that, he flung the bottle of laundry detergent into the basket and clinched the phone. "Hello," he snarled.

"Hullo my dear boy!" Hereford sang into the phone.

"Oh, Hereford. I thought you were Mother. Sorry." Why is he calling me, Parson thought. Odd.

"Wondering why I'm calling?" Hereford chuckled. People were so predictable. "Well, I am, of course calling to see about the progress on the Plan. This is very important to me, you know."

Parson, feeling just a teensy bit hateful, replied, "Frankly, Hereford, there is no progress. I am so desperate I'm actually considering teaching you how to play bridge." Parson snickered a little to himself and continued, "Seriously though, what I really need is to be able to access the main computer again." His neck spasmed as the words crossed his thin lips, and he realized that he had made a significant error in judgment. His little joke to himself had cost him his concentration. Until now, Hereford had had no idea that Parson was behind the appearance of that splashy bridge hand at the sectional.

"So that was you, old shoe," Hereford crooned approvingly. Encouraged by his partner's feat of ingenuity and resourcefulness, he continued: "Well I'll be damned. I should have known that. Never would have expected you to be so ostentatious, though, about your hand choice. A little overdone, don't you think, Pars?"

Hereford relished any opportunity to needle Parson, and that it was about one of his precious little schemes was icing on the cake. Hereford knew that Parson rated his own intelligence far superior to anyone else's. Hereford, needless to say, did not share this flight of fancy. Parson was annoyed with himself. He should've let that rotten phone ring and the devil with Mother. It was her fault, when you got right down to it.

"Son, I can tell that you're a little dismayed at the moment," Hereford continued, "but don't be. Luck's lasting smile has found its way to your weary old predicament. I believe I have the solution for your conundrum." Saving the day was one of Hereford's favorite pastimes, especially when someone was going to owe him for it later.

Parson, being far more concerned about the immediate future than the future future, would gladly owe later for useful information now. From this vantage point, any embarrassment Parson may have had rolled right off his back. He was cheered with the prospect of help in this situation, and congratulated himself silently for really stepping in it this time. "What have you got for me?" Parson asked, dropping his voice for no particular reason.

"For you, I have an in to that computer," Hereford drew out each word.

"Who is it?" Parson grasped.

"Ahem," Hereford cleared his throat, knowing that every moment of delay was torture for Parson. "Some weeks ago, I stopped by to see Vanessa. She mentioned that her new hire, Jenny—"

"Penny," Parson interjected impatiently.

"Oooh, yes, yes. That's right. Penny. I think I was thinking of an old college buddy's daughter . . ."

Parson sighed loudly and tapped the phone.

"Oh, of course. Penny. Well anyway. She used to work for the National Bridge League, in their computer room. I gather she had a great deal of responsibility there. Probably full access. Seems, in fact, that there is a great probability that she was fired as a direct result of your little adventure into their system." Hereford felt pleased.

"Hmm," Parson acknowledged. "This could be useful," he said aloud, rather more to himself than Hereford. "Listen, Herf, I gotta go. I have a feeling that Mother is going to be stopping by, and I have to go get half-and-half for her coffee. She hates milk." Parson felt the rush of his mental wheels grinding into action.

"Okay m'boy. Good luck. Keep me posted." Hereford clicked off the phone and whistled to himself. *That boy's got a real problem with his mother*, he thought.

Parson jiggled his body downstairs to the laundry room. He was pleasantly surprised that there was only one other person using the machines. Without thinking twice, he loaded the contents of his basket into the remaining machines and set out for the corner store to get half-and-half. He got back just in time to see the front door closing behind Mother as she made her way to the elevator. She has a key to my apartment, he thought, let her use it. He headed down to check on his laundry.

By the time he got back to his apartment, Mother had filled every molecule of air with her presence. Her large presiding figure was bent over the small gas stove. She was futilely rearranging the Pyrex containers, trying to achieve the impossible dream of 1963: Happiness from hot, nourishing entrees, placed in the center of the table at the same time, as a meal. She was convinced that her failure to master this skill was the sole cause of her husband's disappearance a number of years ago, and had been trying to remedy the situation three times a day ever since. It had made for a somewhat challenging childhood for Parson, and the challenge had only grown in the last twenty-five years.

"Am I to guess that you didn't get that raise yet, Peanut? I mean, I had expected a new oven this week," she looked up from the overflowing Happy Pyrex that would add a new layer of drips to the oven floor. "Maybe I'm expecting too much, right now?" she added, trying to cloak her iron-fisted judgment.

What Mother failed to realize was that she hardly needed to waste her breath in speaking to him. All she had to do was look—no, all she really had to do was *be* there. Just her presence reminded him of his failure as a human being. In the realm of condemnation and judgment, she was a Life Master. One night, when the computer was on the blink, Parson had analyzed his entire relationship with Mother. He established that the whole messy thing could be reduced to a list of questions. It began with "Why do you insist on calling me that stupid name from childhood (Peanut)?" touched on "Why do you insist on coming over here all the time and bringing me food?" followed closely by, "Why do you always complain about the oven?" raced past "Why do I allow this?" and stopped abruptly at "What's to stop me from killing you today?" Parson was proud of himself for saving all that money on psychotherapy. And while he had come up with no answers, he had at least acknowledged his fear of grabbing her neck and squeezing it until she was very, very quiet. He never did, though, and he was also aware that this omission only added to his feelings of impotence. Killing her would clearly be one of his greatest accomplishments. The only greater feat would be to procure her love. Parson's eyes, though, were always focused on practicality, and he knew that love was beyond the realm of possibility. So he handled it the way of any red-blooded American: he endured and dreamed of being rich.

"Mother," he hissed impatiently, "each of the last four times you have asked me about the oven, I have told you the same thing. You don't remember it, do you?" he scolded.

She looked at him, feeling a slight thrill that she could still make him angry. "I guess not, Peanut," she poked.

"Okay," he was thoroughly exasperated with her. "For the last time: I have to win that pair event with Hereford. I'm still working on a plan. But meanwhile, I have to woo a young woman."

Mother's eyes wandered off to a worn pea-colored pillow stuffed in the corner of the couch. She was bored by her son's needs, especially needs regarding young women.

Parson recognized Mother's sudden apathy as the beginning of a good, long sulk. She was probably upset that he snapped at her, and in lieu of an apology (which he predicted would turn into a big, emotional scene), he offered her one better—to participate in his life. Usually this brought her right out of her sulk, so he forged ahead, revealing his thoughts. "This woman," he looked furtively over to Mother, "is the key to my raise." Parson held her eyes for just a moment longer to impart the seriousness of his words. "How to woo her . . . well, I guess it'll come to me—soon, I hope." Having dropped the bait at her feet, he nonchalantly rose and headed for the door to check his laundry. It would not be long; he knew that she loved to give her opinion, especially if it was about his life.

"Well it just doesn't surprise me at all that you haven't the foggiest notion of what to do here. How could you? Your father could not understand women for the life of him. You have no idea because you have very little masculinity, so dealing with women doesn't come naturally to you, Peanut. Not your fault at all, though, that's not what I'm saying. You have your father to thank for that. Still, I'm here and thank God for that, right? But I'm off the course. This girl, what do you know about her?"

What Parson had viewed as an elegant tactical maneuver was turning out like the Bay of Pigs. He tried to retreat but it was too late. He hadn't wanted her opinion—it was nearly worthless—so he wasn't about to prattle on about details. His clumsy evasions annoyed Mother; she thought he was simply stupid. Void of any real details, Mother sipped her creamy coffee silently. She shifted her large mass uncomfortably in the chair. Finally, she was able to pass gas, and a look of relief washed over her yellowish face. Parson was disgusted, but he dared not say a word. He would vacuum and sterilize the chair seat later. Mother was pensive. Parson needed to put his laundry in the dryer. More than that, he needed to get outside for a breath of stifling summer air to clear out his lungs. As he moved towards the door, she blurted, "I have it! Sit down." It was as though she had been waiting for him to make a move.

"Yes, Mother. I'm listening. I knew you'd come up with something," he pandered. *God, let this be over soon*, Parson thought to himself.

"Well, you have no natural charm," she started in with no fear of reprisal. She had him right where she wanted him. He had to listen. He needed her to be his mother and these were her terms. "And no natural good looks. Your personality is drab at best. You have no hobbies. But, you are a good bridge player. And since that's what you have, that's what you have to use." Her rancor sliced open a slab of thick air.

He hated her. He hated the overcooked mush dripping in his oven. He hated Sunday. He would eat the burnt mush, and he would take her abuse. For that, he hated himself. And he hated her more for hating himself. Choking on his hate, he could barely hear her rattling off her doltish instructions, "Just approach her. Give her a compliment. Ask her to play bridge with you—she will. Be respectful of her. Remember the conversations you have with her and refer to them the next time you see her. Look her in the eyes when you talk to her. She'll be eating out of your hand." Beaten, Parson crept into the basement.

Mojo

Endless hours in Vanessa's club had left Penny strained, drained, and on the verge of a summer cold. Her lower back ached, her right temple was beginning to throb, and the only thing that could hold her attention was the large mug precariously perched on the precipice of the desk. One door slam or loud scream from Vanessa and it was all over. She waited, hanging her eyes wearily on the mug.

"Excuse me." A soft, kind voice filtered through her daze. Penny looked up, and scanned the face for recognition.

"You look very familiar to me, but I'm sorry, I'm pretty new here and I haven't learned everyone's name yet," she apologized. This was the worst part of being in a new job, she thought. It seemed like she had just seen this man a few days ago, but then again, it was a bridge club; she had just seen everybody a few days ago.

"Oh, everybody around here calls me Parson," Parson said comfortably. "I play with Hereford Willis. Once in a while we play a set match against Vanessa," he said affably, hoping to stir her memory. She was prettier than he had remembered. She was also well put together and trim. But, she was a woman, he reminded himself, and she probably had that smart thing going, so he had better watch himself. Perspicacity, they called it.

"Yes, of course," she remembered. "Nice of you to stop by. Are you meeting Hereford here today, or someone else?" she wasted no time in driving to the obvious question.

"No, actually." And sensing her no-nonsense attitude, Parson spontaneously changed his entire plan. He decided to go with the direct route. "Actually, Hereford mentioned to me that you used to work for the NBL."

She nodded.

"I am having some trouble with them, and if you will forgive my boldness, I was hoping you could give me some pointers on how to deal with them." He had become the consummate gentleman.

He was so sincere, she thought, so sweet. Too bad that he wasn't better looking. "What kind of trouble?" she inquired, thankful for the distraction from her work.

"Computer trouble. I can't find the bridge software program that I need. I called them up thinking they would have the solution, but they couldn't help me. You see, I wanted to set up a program to generate specific deals, you know, specific bridge hands. I know they have a system that does that, so I called to ask about it. They were very touchy about the whole subject."

"That doesn't surprise me in the least. That was my department, and it was a very small department. In fact, it was just me, and, as you can see, I'm here," she smiled. It was a smile that had survived earlier setbacks and disappointments—a smile that masked previous betrayals.

"If you don't mind me asking, why are you here and not there?" Parson asked with poised voice.

"On a fluke, really. A while ago—you might have heard about this in the papers—someone broke into the League's main computer system."

"Yes, I did hear about it, though there weren't many details at the time," Parson said calmly.

"Right. No one knows or has been able to trace whoever input that crazy hand into the deal generator that showed up at the Miami sectional. Only three people knew the access code. I, being one of them, got fired." Every time Penny told this story it struck her how ridiculous it was.

"But why do they think that you would do it? What possible motive could you have?" Parson sounded surprised.

"My thoughts exactly. None. My boss didn't see it that way, though. She felt it was a major breach in security," Penny sighed heavily.

"Besides, how do they know that one of the other people didn't do it?" Parson queried casually.

"Well, one of them is my boss and the other is the head computer programmer for the League. But anyway, enough of all that. Back to your original question. Why is it you need a deal generator? Are you going to start an alternative league? Let me know, I'll run it for you," she laughed.

Parson was encouraged by her response; he felt she was receptive to his questions. He plodded forward, "I doubt if I really need a deal generator . . . or at least I doubt I need one as complicated as the League's. What I need is a program that will generate very specific types of hands for my clients and the classes I teach. So if we need practice responding to one notrump, or practice bidding slams, I can make up a bunch of those hands. You get the point. It would be a great advantage with clients." As he talked, he sold himself on the idea.

"I'd be happy to help you where I can. I can't do it now, though," she said sadly.

"No, no. Of course not. But maybe we could get together one afternoon or evening and discuss it. We can make a trade for bridge sessions," he threw the bait out, though it didn't seem like he needed it. It had been a while since Penny had had such a normal and polite one-on-one conversation. The low-key speaker was charming, intelligent and valued her professional expertise and judgment. As always, she was too kind and too battered to say no to sincere flattery.

"Okay. Sounds great to me. Give me your number and I'll call you later on in the week when I know my schedule," she smiled enthusiastically.

Penny's day brightened. Zealously finishing her work, she headed over to the Tick-Tock Coffee Shop. Meyer, Ford and Richie haunted the place, and she knew they would be hanging out having coffee. She strolled in and scanned the booths. She spied them roosting in a red vinyl booth, clucking like three hens. As she arrived at the table, Ford stood up. "There goes Ford, making me look bad," Richie quipped. He had had a crush on Penny for eons.

"So, how was Vanessa the Contessa today, comrade?" Meyer's question was followed by a chorus of laughter. Penny looked immediately to Richie, and was relieved to see that he was laughing, too.

"Yeah, you didn't tell me your new job was hand-maiden to a Contessa? Very prestigous," Richie winked.

"I was trying to, but you virtually hung up on me. Remember? So, no, I didn't call you back and tell you," Penny was chagrinned, "but I thought you were calling me back."

"Best defense is a good offense," chimed Ford.

"Hey, Vanessa is no fool. She got a good hire. I just wish I had been in the position to hire you myself," Richie smiled.

"And as soon as you are, I expect a phone call," Penny flashed a big grin.

"I'll just come and pick you up," Richie flirted.

"Oh God, enough. He'll park the white horse in the front. When are you two going to just go out and forget all of this friend stuff. What's the point of it, anyway?" Meyer mocked.

"I'm ignoring you, Meyer," Penny said and changed the subject. "I have an interesting story for you three."

"The Contessa was beheaded in the Revolution?" Richie said hopefully.

"Ford perked up at that prospect," Meyer said.

"No, not that I know of. But I do have her bound and gagged in the basement, Penny joked. I have a piped-in recording of a voice reciting every convention known to man, over and over and over. It's the most satisfying torture I could think of: She is sitting in a corner, listening to conventions, gnashing her teeth."

"How much do I have to pay to watch?" Ford drawled.

"Why, in fact, Mr. Maddox," Meyer put on his best car salesman voice, equipped with inflection, "not only do you not have to pay anything, *she'll* pay *you!* That's the beauty of the thing. She'll sit across the table from you, listen to conventions and gnash her teeth. Your lucky day."

"The next time I need to remember my past life as a tortured Christian in a Roman stadium, I'll call you," Ford parleyed.

"Actually," Penny dropped her voice and squashed her eyes into slits, "one of the local bridge pros stopped by to see me today. It's a mystery. Guess who."

"Did he have greasy hair?" Ford asked.

"I believe it's styling gel," she scolded.

"Gel? It's bad hygiene. How 'bout his breath? Does he use that gel on his teeth?" Ford's dancing eyes glittered with glee.

"Are those his teeth? Geez, you'd never know. I thought he mugged a ventriloquist's dummy for those clackers," Meyer joined in.

"He *is* a ventriloquist's dummy. I just haven't figured out where Hereford puts his hand to make him talk." A wry smile slid across Ford's face.

"Maybe, Ford, the topic of body odor and cleanliness should not be broached here. Seems the little lady is fond of perspiration. Perhaps he introduced her to his pet body lice." The entire table groaned. Richie doubled over laughing watching Penny turn green.

"Basically," Ford said, not missing a beat, "you're annoyed because we know who it is. You didn't even get to have any fun. We all know what that stern,

I'm-going-to-defend-the-person-who-doesn't-bathe look means. We know that your charities don't include Save The Individual Noxious Kind, known to insiders as S.T.I.N.K. We also know, having checked all of your references, that you do not have any friends who are Hygienically Challenged. We gotcha." Ford, the last great straight man, broke into laughter.

"So what did he want?" Meyer's voice took a serious turn.

"Oh, nothing really. It seemed he just stopped by to say hi. He seems like a very nice person. And he didn't smell," she said slightly defensively.

"He's up to something then, because he never bathes on weekdays," Ford said.

"I take it from all this that he does not make your top 100 list," Penny said.

"He does. Top 100 slimeballs. On that list he is, oh, maybe, number one," Meyer confirmed.

"He was very pleasant to me," Penny insisted.

"Sure he was," Meyer said.

"And what man wouldn't be—," Richie added.

"What did he want?" Meyer diligently returned to the question at hand, yet to be answered.

"Forget it. He didn't want anything. You guys are obviously not going to give him a chance," Penny said obstinately. Men could be so foolish.

"We've all known him a long time," Meyer said reasonably. "He's just not a swell guy, Penny."

Richie took up the sword. "So what did he want, anyway?"

"He asked me a couple of computer questions. I'm going to help him set up a program on his computer in exchange for some bridge sessions," Penny stated matter-of-factly.

"Excuse me, I'm going to be sick," Meyer said. "What's wrong with that? It's a fair trade. All right. I'm going now."

"Penny, I haven't known you that long, but I've known you long enough to say don't do it. The guy is a scum and he wants something from you," Ford said earnestly.

"You mean sex, right? You are such men, all of you together. He can't just be interested in knowing me, or that I might know something professionally that he's interested in?" This was very frustrating to Penny.

"No one said anything about sex, Penny. If the truth be told, I think it's very unlikely that that's what he wants. If it was just sex, it would be easy," Meyer analyzed.

She shot him a look.

"Oh, well, not that you're easy. Good God. I meant, easy to see his motive," Meyer scrambled.

"The question is, what then," Richie puzzled.

"I'm going. I'll let you know."

"Come on, Penny, don't leave. We won't talk about him any more," Richie cajoled.

"Yeah, like I don't know Meyer and all of his questions," Penny smirked.

"She's got a point there," Ford agreed. "Meyer this is all your fault."

"Right-o. My fault that my little buddy here has lost her mind and is up-in-arms over some spineless . . . I think she's just mad enough that she's taking it personally," Meyer quipped.

"That's right, I am, so wait 'til I leave. I will see all of you boys, ahem, later. Adios, amigos."

The three amigos were left to silently watch her car pull out of the parking lot. Richie was the first to speak. "What does that cockroach want with Penny, huh? And what would possess her to set up a computer program for him, I'd like to know."

"I wouldn't worry too much about her there, Rich. She's solid. He somehow has her hoodwinked, or he's trying to," Meyer said calmly.

"It seemed like she was looking forward to doing that favor for him, I think," Richie lamented.

"Naa. She was just defending herself. Don't waste energy thinking about that. Let's figure out what Parson's agenda is," Meyer said, pragmatism showing. "Let's see. One obvious possibility is that it has something to do with Vanessa and her club . . ."

Overcome by a flash of brilliance, Richie interrupted: "Maybe Parson wants to get Vanessa as a client. Think about it—the last time he played against you two, he must have seen the strain in the Contessa-Maddox partnership. From what I heard, the performance got rave reviews: 'Vigorous dialogue, Compelling action, Promise of more to come.' He undoubtedly thinks this client is ripe for the picking, so he's hanging around the back gate of the garden, whispering in Eve's ear." Richie, who had very little time in his life for theorizing, was pretty darn proud of his theory, especially for an off-the-cuff kind of thing. He sat beaming, waiting for kudos.

"No, he already has Hereford. A dictator in the hand is worth two in the bush. Plus, two full-time clients is too many," Meyer stated. Richie's face fell flat.

"Yeah, two too many if it's those two," Ford snorted.

"I think Ford's job is getting to him," Richie chuckled.

"Hell, Ford's job is getting to me. It's all he talks about," Meyer quipped, adding an exaggerated eye-roll for emphasis. Then, in a more serious tone, "By the way, Ford, speaking of your job, I ran into your erstwhile employer and his wife outside Cineplex 3 last night. I said hello to him for you, and he seemed embarrassed."

"Ashenfelter?" Ford questioned.

"The very same," answered Meyer.

"He was supposed to be doing the global tour with his wife. That's how I ended up getting stuck with Vanessa."

"Why in the world would he lie to you?" Meyer wondered out loud.

"I smell Hereford's foul scent mixed up in this business. I figured he was behind it. He's had it in for me since the day I was born."

"It sure looks that way," Meyer confirmed.

"Okay guys," Richie said impatiently. "Let's get back to Parson and Penny."

"You're right," Meyer agreed, "first things first. Let's summarize what we have: basically, Hereford's behind it, but we don't know why, or Parson's in it on his own, and we still don't know why. So we don't know who's behind it or why, or even if it exists in the first place."

"In other words," Ford concluded, "we have nothing."

"Right . . . well, there's a point there. But, we've got to figure it out before that guy works his mojo on her," Meyer urged.

"Mojo?" Ford asked, wondering where Meyer was taking the conversation now.

"You know, magic, like a spell. And that guy, as disgusting as he is, can work magic on normally sane, rational people. I've never been able to figure out how he does it."

"I don't know either, but he's done it here. We've spent thirty minutes on this guy and ended up with nothing. Let's go," Ford said impatiently.

* * * * * * * * *

As Penny stepped through the door into Parson's apartment, she felt the strong, tight hand of claustrophobia grip her chest. Coughing, she struggled for a moment to breathe. "Excuse me," she apologized, "must be allergies."

"Oh," Parson said haughtily, "I know there's a lot of stuff in here. I'm a collector." Penny, happy to be breathing again, regained her natural curiosity.

"What do you collect?" she asked brightly, walking into the dim living room.

"Collections. I collect collections of things," Parson sniffed with a finality that concluded the issue. Penny surveyed the room and speculated that the walls had not been seen in a decade. The shelves reached from floor to ceiling, stretching the length of the walls. Barely visible, the shelves were like pack mules, so heavily burdened it was a wonder they didn't collapse under the weight. Mostly, the items were housed in boxes with meticulously affixed labels. There were the usual collectibles: the pre-1980 campaign pins, Republican only; the group of tiger-eye agates, but only one of each size; and moths mounted on black felt, propped in front of a mausoleum box which entombed their comrades, themselves patiently awaiting display. Then there were some unusual variations, like a rather large collection of spotted tree-frog bones, with one frog reconstructed in front of its box, and what appeared to be several hundred cigarette butts, smoked almost to the filter, all kissed by a trace of lipstick. These, too, were mounted in small cases on a black felt background; the less important ones were individually shrink wrapped and filed into boxes. The boxes were labeled Sunset Boulevard, August, 1969. Penny felt the unwelcome return of the claustrophobia, and decided she didn't really want to know too much about these collections after all.

Parson, aware of the impact of his collectibles upon the noncollector, began chatting animatedly about computers, bridge and life. Penny was halfway through a cup of tea before her quiet horror subsided. Relieved, she could now focus on actually hearing the words coming out of Parson's mouth.

At last, Parson's monologue paused long enough for Penny to suggest: "Let's see what we can work out for you on your computer."

"Great idea," Parson said giddily, nervous with anticipation. They sat down in front of the computer, located tantalizingly close to the only window in the room. The window (except for the top of the frame) was, however, entirely enveloped by a dense brown cloth that hung leadenly to the floor, the bottom half disappearing behind labeled boxes. Penny guessed that the window, like the walls, had not been seen or heard from in some time now.

"I know you are interested in the generator that the League has," she began, "but you may be able to do what you want to do with a lot less trouble. There are a couple of pretty good deal generators on the market, and they sell for about $49.95. One of those might be just what you need. Someone's done all the work for you." Penny was happy to keep her word and help him, but, given the opportunity, she would have bolted like lightning.

The years of grudging coexistence with an insatiably demanding mother had, in the end, stood Parson in good stead. While trying to please her, he had developed an uncanny acumen that could sense a shifting mood like a Richter scale. People, and how to work them, had become a science for him. So, when he heard the pin-drop of hesitation in Penny's voice, he realized something was amiss and immediately changed his course of action.

Parson softened his voice and his body, trying to present a relaxed demeanor. "Yes, I looked at those," he said, having prepared himself for all the possible discussions of hand generators, "but I don't think they will meet my needs. They seem very limited. But," he continued, not leaving her any room to escape, "I'll understand if you have changed your mind and don't feel like doing this." He lowered his eyes forlornly. "You know, it's kind of funny. I usually don't have people over to my place for just this reason. They are uncomfortable because I'm different from the majority of people."

Embarrassed by the precision of his truth, Penny laughed self-consciously.

He continued: "When people meet me, they like me. Then they see that I am content to live alone. They wonder. Then they discover that my hobbies are somewhat unusual. They wonder. After that, well," he sighed and shook his head, "most often they don't give me a chance. They write me off as a nerd or a freak. As a result, I don't socialize much. No occasion to hang around with bridge players, or anyone else, for that matter. It doesn't bother me too much—I mean, it does in this case because you seem like such a quality person, intelligent and able to think for yourself—because I know that I'm an original and independent person. I know that most people cannot accept the way that I am. That's okay; originality is very threatening to people. For some reason, it is particularly threatening to men." In saying this, he had baited the trap. Parson backed off to give his mark some space to consider. There were no guarantees at this point.

As if by magic, Penny simultaneously felt sympathy, guilt, and complimented. She understood him completely. She, too, had been the victim of that provincial thinking; unfairly judged on her lifestyle choices. And she felt guilty that she had fallen into judging Parson, and even more guilty that she had disappointed him. With a new ease, Penny opened the gates and unleashed a flood of conversation. Parson had guessed right—these chords resonated for her. Thank God for his demanding mother. Parson was in control now. He let the conversation percolate for a while, suggested take-out food for a light dinner, and with a hunter's timing, circled his prey.

"So, Penny, what exactly did happen with your job?" his voice keeping with the casual cadence of the conversation. "It doesn't make any sense to me that you were fired."

"Me neither," she swallowed and gave a little laugh. "I still don't believe it. The whole thing is ridiculous."

"Do you mind talking about it?" he asked with concern.

"No, no not at all. I don't understand it, really. I got to work Monday morning and my boss called me in and told me that someone had accessed our computer system. I didn't know anything about it, and honestly, I didn't think it was such a big deal. We're not the F.B.I."

The mere thought of the F.B.I. or any investigator made Parson queasy. "Why did your boss think it was a big deal then?" he asked calmly.

"Because, she said that the public would think that all the events were rigged, or could be," Penny said, helping herself to more Kung Po chicken from the tin.

"You don't think so?" he probed gingerly.

"Do we have any more soy sauce?" she shuffled through the paper bag. "Hmm. Do you mean do I think the events can be rigged or do I think the public would perceive them that way?" She squirted the inky liquid onto her rice.

"Both questions, I guess. I hadn't thought about it," he lied. Parson looked down at his food. The conversation was travelling a little closer to his interests than he liked.

"Yeah, I s'pose the events could be rigged, but why would they? Who would do that, you know, and why would anyone do it?" To her, this whole line of thought was crazy. "What would be the point? You would know that you cheated and didn't really win, so what satisfaction would you get?"

How moral conviction stifles one's imagination, Parson thought to himself. Once in a blue moon, he had the desire to lay the truth out for somebody who was missing a big piece. Not for any cruelty's sake, but just to let them taste another slice of life. That desire was with him now. He wanted to say, "People would rig an event to win. Simply to win. Winning means a lot to a lot of people for a lot of reasons. People would rig an event because they can, for the sheer power of it all. And, why not?" But instead of offering her his mincemeat pie of life, he reached for more eggplant with garlic sauce. Safer and more practical. "The last time the computer was accessed, what was the point?" he asked evenly, revealing none of his thoughts.

"I don't know about the last time, but the only time I know of was when someone input a hand. I think it was done as a joke. I didn't take it altogether too seriously. It was a goofy hand from a bridge book. *The Pack* or something like that." This topic annoyed her.

"Oh yeah," Parson feigned recollection. "I saw it in the paper. It was a deal from *Right Through the Pack*."

"That's right. All the hearts were in the same hand. It was obviously a prank. There was no point to it, really."

"I'm surprised the person got into the system. I imagine that the League's computer is protected," he led. "In fact, I'd like to have a code like theirs to protect this new system we set up so there are no worries of anyone breaking in," he smiled.

"We can try, but honestly, I don't know if I can do that. That system is protected, and I'm not even quite sure how the code is generated. I do know that every quarter it automatically regenerates itself." Penny felt like she should know more, but she didn't have to use the code any more and she couldn't have cared less, really, how the code was generated.

"Why do they do it that way? Then they have to give out the code again every three months. That doesn't seem very practical." Parson was baffled.

"Well, there were only three people who knew the code, and one of them was me. The other two wrote the program that creates it. It's a fail-safe system."

"Because you have to know the algorithm used to generate it," Parson checked.

"Exactly," Penny confirmed. "It's based on bridge. It has something to do with bidding sequences and the date."

"That's clever. It seems, though, that since we don't know the whole system, it would be difficult to implement it in my computer. Hmm, I'm thinking that maybe we should come up with something else. What do you think?" Parson wanted to start wrapping things up. He believed he had gotten all the information she had. It was not as much as he had hoped, but it was enough to go on. From this point, he assumed he could work it out; the pressing question now being, could he work it out in time for the Blue Ribbon Pairs.

The evening wore on, and Parson tied up the loose laces of the social shoe. As a rule of thumb, he felt that the art to hustling was allowing your marks to keep their illusions, i.e., they should never know they're being taken advantage of. A further footnote for novices: take particular care with women. They are clearly more aware of people than their male counterparts, and quite a few of them are pretty smart, too. Don't let one discover you; women can be ruthless enemies.

Parson donned the attitude of a gentleman and walked Penny to her car. He thanked her profusely for all of her help.

"I really don't feel as though I've helped you much at all," said Penny, disappointed with herself. "We didn't get that system together. You are no better off than you were."

"Oh but I am, trust me. I definitely appreciate it," Parson softly assured her. "All we have to do is schedule the time for the bridge sessions. Your convenience."

"I couldn't take your time for that. I really didn't do anything," Penny protested shyly.

"A deal's a deal, and I never go back on my word," he oozed, gazing into her eyes. He squeezed her hand lightly and smiled with his soft-sell eyes. "It's starting to sprinkle. Get in so you don't get wet."

"Yes. Okay, then, I'll call you tomorrow to see if we can find a good time for both of us." He is thoughtful, she said to herself.

"Great. If there's no answer, keep trying. My answering machine is broken," he said.

"Okay!" she sounded cheered as she thanked him for dinner and got into the car.

Mother would be pleased, Parson thought to himself, but decided not to tell her. He would tell her the contrary: that he took her advice and the evening was a failure. He would darkly prophesy that he would lose his job, letting the implications of that hang in the air. Let her suffer. Let her think him a failure and suffer because of it. She made him. Here, guilt was no mere two-way street; it was an eight-lane highway.

Driving through the oppressive darkness, Penny noticed that it had started to pour. The gusting wind bullied her little car all over the road. This was no sprinkle. This was a full-fledged Miami storm that was heading for hurricane status. *I don't remember a storm warning*, she thought nervously, and turned on the radio.

115

The Gilded Ass

Pulling into Trumps' parking lot, Ford saw Hereford's car, Parson's car and Vanessa's car parked side by side, lining the entrance. He checked his watch to see if he was late (he wasn't), and parked his own vehicle in the center of the lot. Faced with these three vultures, Ford did not even have a thin thread of optimism to mend his tattered hope for a pleasant bridge match. His only consolation was that Time was a relative thing. His life was long and good, and even if this set match was bad, it was short relative to his life.

Braced with a warrior's resolve, he entered the building, grabbed his sweater from the closet, and strode fearlessly to the private room in the rear of the club. There he found Hereford and Parson, a huddled puddle, awash with the low tones of a *really* important conversation. Ignoring them, Ford walked to the window where he stood gazing.

Bored with the view of the parking lot, his mind fell to musing on the irony of freezing to death in late summer, in Miami. This was an event, he thought, that would reach epidemic proportions here at Trumps. Ford pictured people quietly freezing to death as they sat holding their cards. Ford was planning a coup d'etât of the cooling system when Vanessa teetered in, swaying gently atop her spindly heels. She flashed her best hostess smile, and with perfectly poised attentiveness, she said, "Hereford, Parson, so glad you could join us today. Can I get you anything?"

Hereford locked his piercing eyes on hers and replied, "Yes, Vanessa, you could get us a good bridge game." The sharp challenge of his graceless humor sliced the air. Ford quietly turned toward the battle, watching. Vanessa dropped her smile on the floor and stared at him in disbelief. "Perhaps you want to up the stakes on this match?" Her stiletto voice stabbed each word with articulation. Hereford calmly leaned back and shifted his focus to Ford's face. He searched for weakness in the familiar eyes. But years of rubber bridge matches had left Ford's face a smooth stone of inscrutability. His silent blue eyes revealed nothing. Inside, Ford giggled. Hell, maybe this'll make her play better.

"Vanessa, my Contessa," Hereford drawled in his most patronizing voice. "How about two dollars a point? That would make a vulnerable grand slam worth over $4,000. Or would those stakes jeopardize the goose that laid your golden egg, my dear?"

"Oh Hereford, please, those are paltry stakes," she threw him off with a deliciously dismissive wave. "We both know that I'm worth far more than you are."

Hmm, Ford calculated, unless he's changed, Hereford will find that remark pretty intolerable coming from a woman. Looks like I have a front row seat to what promises to be the battle of the month. *The champion ego, who remains after many decades, the undefeated superman of the asinine. The challenger, weighing in at a mere ninety-one pounds soaking wet, is small but has an ego made of kryptonite. There's the bell . . .*

Vanessa placed her cappuccino precisely on her corner of the table and sat down. Hereford shuffled and dealt one deck of cards while Parson shuffled the other. Vanessa picked up each card as it was dealt, fitting it neatly into her hand. Methodically, she sorted and re-sorted her cards, counting and planning. Hereford stealthily studied his opponent. He watched her lips moving noiselessly as she counted her points, and when he was absolutely sure she was thoroughly involved in her hand, he said, gruffly and purposely, "Vanessa, move your coffee, dear. I am afraid it will spill."

"Well, if it spills, dear, I will have it cleaned up," she snapped without so much as a glance toward her coffee. Parson looked over to Ford, who returned his look.

"Yes, Vanessa, I am quite sure you would have it cleaned up, but that won't help at all if it spills on my new silk trousers," Hereford insisted.

"I have never spilled a cappuccino in my life and that, my dear, speaks volumes. It will not spill," she re-torted, taking the bait. Crossing her legs under the table, she pulled on the long, gold ropes that draped between her silicone vestiges of youth. She refocused on her hand.

Hereford dogged her. "I think it's really unsports-manlike for you to try to distract me by keeping your coffee on the edge of the table like that. It's an unfair advantage for you. I'm busy worrying about your bloody coffee spilling on my pants," he badgered.

Vanessa exasperatedly closed her hand and slammed it palm down on the table. "As for the pants, I'll buy you a new pair. And as for what's in them, I simply can't imagine that there's much worth worrying about," she finished with a flourish. Strangely, both

Ford and Parson were simultaneously stricken with what's known as Professional Asphyxiation. This condition primarily afflicts employees. It is temporary, but can be hazardous to the wallet, if not immediately controlled. It is caused by laughter that tries to get out of the body, but is choked back by the wise mind that wants to keep collecting the old paycheck. Bosses hate to be laughed at.

Vanessa looked at her hand again, but her thoughts were on Hereford and the coffee. Why he had waited until the last possible moment to bring all this up, she would never understand. And, really, if it meant that much to him, he should have simply moved the coffee himself. Ridiculous. She frowned, trying to remember what she was thinking about before Hereford had started all this nonsense about his pants.

Vanessa gave it a good fight, but she did not have the same powers of concentration that Hereford did. Hereford's gamesmanship had worked perfectly. She could not easily move from wrangling with Hereford into playing bridge.

Hereford had dealt himself:

♠ Q 6 5 3 2
♡ K Q J
♢ K 2
♣ K Q J

Looking at a balanced 17-count, Hereford wavered. With a carrot and a stick, Parson had trained Hereford never to open notrump; Parson thought that Hereford's declaring a hand was like a guy off the street performing back surgery. Hereford knew this, knew the results supported Parson, and found it annoying. Why should he pay Parson to have all the fun? Hell, Parson should be able to win anyway, even if his mother were declaring. Hereford smiled to himself, ignored the possible one-spade opening, and opened one notrump.

Vul: None
Dlr: East

FORD
♠ K 4
♡ —
◇ Q J 9 8 7 6
♣ A 9 7 6 5

PARSON
♠ 8 7
♡ A 10 8 4 2
◇ 10 5
♣ 8 4 3 2

HEREFORD
♠ Q 6 5 3 2
♡ K Q J
◇ K 2
♣ K Q J

VANESSA
♠ A J 10 9
♡ 9 7 6 5 3
◇ A 4 3
♣ 10

WEST	NORTH	EAST	SOUTH
PARSON	FORD	HEREFORD	VANESSA
—	—	1NT	Pass
2◇ (Alert*)	Double	2♡	2♠
Pass	3♣	Pass	3♠
All Pass			

* = transfer

After Hereford's one notrump, Vanessa was still trying to collect her mind. She hesitated a moment, and passed. Parson, with his chin dragging toward his chest,

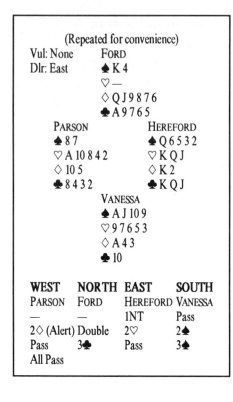

(Repeated for convenience)

Vul: None
Dlr: East

FORD
♠ K 4
♡ —
◇ Q J 9 8 7 6
♣ A 9 7 6 5

PARSON
♠ 8 7
♡ A 10 8 4 2
◇ 10 5
♣ 8 4 3 2

HEREFORD
♠ Q 6 5 3 2
♡ K Q J
◇ K 2
♣ K Q J

VANESSA
♠ A J 10 9
♡ 9 7 6 5 3
◇ A 4 3
♣ 10

WEST	NORTH	EAST	SOUTH
PARSON	FORD	HEREFORD	VANESSA
—	—	1NT	Pass
2◇ (Alert)	Double	2♡	2♠
Pass	3♣	Pass	3♠
All Pass			

bid two diamonds. Hereford brusquely stated that Parson's bid was a transfer to two hearts. Vanessa snatched her head up and narrowed her eyes skeptically. "Isn't he supposed to just say 'alert?'" she questioned the table.

"Well," Ford replied calmly, hoping to relieve her anxiety, "that's the way it used to be. They changed the rules recently. Now, it is just noted as 'Transfer.' It's just semantics; no big deal, really."

"This is exactly the problem in bridge today. There are simply too many conventions. This, Mr. Maddox, is why I don't like to play conventions," Vanessa snapped. "I'm a natural player," she reminded him.

"A natural something," Hereford answered.

Here we go, Ford thought to himself, but I am paying my bills. "I am paying my bills" had become the mantra Ford used to soothe his nerves. With a calm mind again, he doubled. Hereford bid two hearts, and just when it seemed to Ford that things were moving along swimmingly, his partner bid an alarming two

122

spades. Ford was perplexed, to say the least. His mind seized the problem with both hands and tried to untie the knots quickly. Did Vanessa realize that his double showed diamonds? If she couldn't bid over one notrump in the first place, why was she bidding spades now? Maybe she thought he was making a takeout double—no, surely after Hereford bid two hearts she would have realized that that was impossible. Ford, knowing he left his psychic powers at home on the kitchen counter, rapidly concluded that Vanessa in two spades was no picnic and he had better become the declarer posthaste. He showed his second suit by bidding three clubs, and ignored the confusion that clouded the Contessa's face.

She paused and looked at him a moment, furrowed her forehead, and stubbornly refused to give up her hand. She rebid spades, three of them, and Ford realized that this auction could well reach catastrophic proportions before the bidding was done. He ran like a jack rabbit in hunting season, passing before the doubling started, all the while wondering what in the hell she could possibly have in her hand.

Parson led the heart ace and Ford laid the dummy down. Shocked, Vanessa began sucking air, a sound disturbingly similar to a vacuum cleaner with emphysema. The entire table braced for a tirade. She composed herself, though, relieving Ford's tension-filled neck and disappointing Hereford. "Mr. Maddox," she started, still in glassy-eyed shock, "I believe you should have bid diamonds."

"Yes . . . my double showed diamonds," Ford replied, neck-tension returning.

"And how, pray tell, was I to know that double showed diamonds and not takeout?" she asked. Before Ford could reply, she aggressively trumped the heart lead in dummy, and led back an assertive diamond queen for a successful finesse. Drunk with the power of declarer, she reeled off the ace of clubs, ruffed a club, and ruffed a heart with dummy's last trump. Then she ruffed another club, and cashed the diamond ace. At last, as if smoking a cigarette after sex, she paused to admire the thick stack of seven tricks in front of her. She was left with this position, needing just two more tricks for her contract:

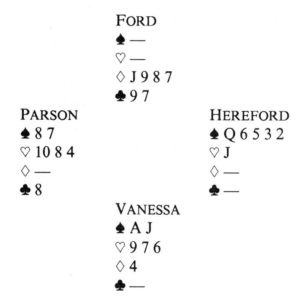

```
                    FORD
                    ♠ —
                    ♡ —
                    ◇ J 9 8 7
                    ♣ 9 7
   PARSON                        HEREFORD
   ♠ 8 7                         ♠ Q 6 5 3 2
   ♡ 10 8 4                      ♡ J
   ◇ —                          ◇ —
   ♣ 8                          ♣ —
                    VANESSA
                    ♠ A J
                    ♡ 9 7 6
                    ◇ 4
                    ♣ —
```

Ford was relieved at this turn of events. It was pretty clear that she was left with the ace-jack of spades, and there was an easy exit into any side suit, whereupon she could eventually score two more trump tricks for the contract and voilà, no disaster. Why she laid down the spade ace at this point, he would never know for sure. Meyer conjectured later that she must have been hoping the queen would drop. "But how could she possibly think that? Not even one round of spades had been played." Ford was wondering if it was one of those "play-by-feel" moments. Meyer only smiled and said that some things were not meant to be understood.

The inevitable came to pass, and Vanessa fell one trick short of her contract. Parson cut the shuffled deck to Vanessa for the next deal. As she started to deal, Ford could see the frustration flowing through Vanessa's veins. Her painted lips pursed sourly, and she stared at an empty spot on the table. The room was still except for the soft swoosh of the cards leaving Vanessa's bony fingers and gliding round the table. She had finished dealing, and as they were picking up their hands, Hereford took the opportunity to placidly remind Vanessa of the score. "That's $100, I believe," he said evenly and began to sort his hand. Ford looked up in time to see his lovely partner's face beginning to distort with anger.

He only caught a glimpse of the redness, though, because of the sudden, extreme neck spasm that closed his eyes in wincing pain. *Good God in Heaven*, he thought, *this is more than I can bear*. "Mr. Maddox, you could have passed two spades," she spat her words across the table. "If you had passed two spades, we would have gone plus." Clinging to the last thread of his frayed rope of professionalism, Ford calmly stated that there were nine tricks if she didn't lay down the spade ace. That said, he focused on his hand, wishing this would all disappear: the players, the cards, the table, the building. But he couldn't shake Vanessa's relentless glower.

Hereford was enjoying himself thoroughly. What a glorious morning, he thought; what a pleasant, invigorating game. And, like an old cat toying with a new mouse, he did not want to kill with the direct attack, so he cloaked his question with a child's innocence, "Parson, doesn't that hand belong in diamonds? I think there was a game in diamonds with that hand? Or am I wrong?"

```
        (Repeated for convenience)
Vul: None   FORD
Dlr: East   ♠ K 4
            ♡ —
            ◇ Q J 9 8 7 6
            ♣ A 9 7 6 5
PARSON              HEREFORD
♠ 8 7              ♠ Q 6 5 3 2
♡ A 10 8 4 2       ♡ K Q J
◇ 10 5             ◇ K 2
♣ 8 4 3 2          ♣ K Q J
            VANESSA
            ♠ A J 10 9
            ♡ 9 7 6 5 3
            ◇ A 4 3
            ♣ 10
```

Taking the cue from his boss, Parson chimed in effusively, "Yes, that hand definitely has a game. A slam, in fact." Parson stopped to adjust his voice, and continued with the authoritative pitch of The Expert, "There are several ways you can make 12 tricks in diamonds. Of course, I'm sure you can see the simplest is to rough two clubs to set up the suit, cash the diamond ace, drive out the diamond king and claim."

Hereford sleazed like a second-rate vamp, "Imagine that, a slam their way and I had a strong notrump."

"By the way," Parson took the opportunity to demonstrate his incredible acumen for the game, "just as a note, Hereford, if I had led a trump against three spades, I don't think she could ever make the hand." "Aaah, yes, true, I see what you mean," Hereford said with a peacock's humility. And then noticing Vanessa's whitened knuckles, he added, "Don't hold the cards so tightly, dear, you're liable to bend them." That Vanessa didn't spontaneously combust was miraculous.

Several deals later, Hereford dealt himself a most powerful 17-count:

Vul: E-W
Dlr: East

```
                    FORD
                    ♠ —
                    ♡ K Q J 6 2
                    ◇ J 8 5 4
                    ♣ K J 10 3
PARSON                              HEREFORD
♠ —                                ♠ A K Q J 9 8 7 6
♡ 10 9 8 7                         ♡ A 4 3
◇ A 9                              ◇ K 3
♣ A Q 9 8 7 5 4                    ♣ —
                    VANESSA
                    ♠ 10 5 4 3 2
                    ♡ 5
                    ◇ Q 10 7 6 2
                    ♣ 6 2
```

WEST	NORTH	EAST	SOUTH
PARSON	FORD	HEREFORD	VANESSA
—	—	1♠	Pass
2♣	2♡	2♠	Pass
3♣	Pass	3NT	Pass
Pass	Double	Redouble	All Pass

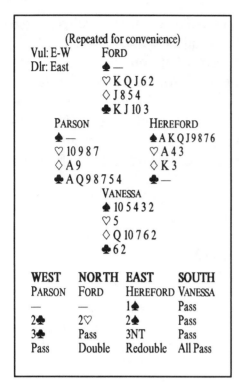

(Repeated for convenience)

Vul: E-W   FORD
Dlr: East   ♠ —
            ♡ K Q J 6 2
            ◊ J 8 5 4
            ♣ K J 10 3

PARSON   HEREFORD
♠ —   ♠ A K Q J 9 8 7 6
♡ 10 9 8 7   ♡ A 4 3
◊ A 9   ◊ K 3
♣ A Q 9 8 7 5 4   ♣ —

            VANESSA
            ♠ 10 5 4 3 2
            ♡ 5
            ◊ Q 10 7 6 2
            ♣ 6 2

WEST	NORTH	EAST	SOUTH
PARSON	FORD	HEREFORD	VANESSA
—	—	1♠	Pass
2♣	2♡	2♠	Pass
3♣	Pass	3NT	Pass
Pass	Double	Redouble	All Pass

His hand organized, Hereford stretched back in his chair a little, picked up his tall glass of water and swirled it, causing the ice to clatter annoyingly against the glass. He didn't drink it though; he just kept swirling it around, clacking the ice. His brain tingled with a mild euphoria. He was content. Blissful, even. His mind happily replayed the scenes of Vanessa erupting, word for word, moment by moment. With each replay, he reached a deeper state of peace with the world. This state, while undoubtedly good for his nervous system, was rather detrimental to the old bridge game. His mind gambolled over the cards counting the points like so many girls at the dance, missing the hand at large. Instead of showing a strong two-bid, he understated his hand by opening one spade.

Parson, seldom subject to the throes of glee, bid the obvious two clubs, followed by Ford's two-heart overcall. Hereford remained distracted through the duration of the auction, and as such, underbid his hand by about fifteen tricks, eventually settling in only three no-trump.

Ford thought about his own hand and this particular type of auction. Experience showed that the penalty double, albeit a slightly speculative action, pays big in the long run. Besides, Ford thought to himself, this is the odds-on choice. The suits rate to be splitting badly, and *sitting* badly. I have clubs behind the dummy, and surely, my partner has spades behind the declarer.

With that, he doubled, and had opened his umbrella in a hurricane. Hereford narrowed his eyes and challenged Ford with an abrupt redouble. Vanessa was hoping to recoup some of her lost money and pride. She led her heart, which Hereford promptly won. He fired out the spade ace. Discovering Ford's void, he tipped his head back and cackled mercilessly.

Turning to Ford, Hereford triumphantly announced the facts like a stay of execution, "How about that! Who would have thought that I could have misbid my hand, had a horrible break in the spade suit, and still be able to make two overtricks in three-notrump redoubled. Nothing less than a miracle."

It will be a miracle if I don't choke you to death before the end of the day, Ford thought, and bit the inside of his cheek hard to keep himself from saying anything. Ford played on in sullen silence while Hereford cleared the spades. Vanessa got in with her spade ten, but she had no heart to play. Regaining the lead, Hereford scooped in his 11 easy tricks. Feigning generosity, Hereford conceded a trick at the end, and began the scoring ritual, calling out, "Three notrump, doubled and redoubled, vulnerable with two overtricks. Let's see, that's

100 times 2 for the double, and doubled again for the redouble is 400. We add 100 for the insult, new scoring, and it's 500 for the game bonus. Okay, so far that's 400 + 100 + 500 for 1,000," he smiled at Vanessa, who was definitely not smiling back, "and now let's see, Miss Contessa. Those overtricks. They are worth 400 each, bringing our total on this one hand to 1,800. Unusual number, wouldn't you say, Parson?" Hereford stretched his smile across his face.

"Pretty unusual," Parson confirmed.

"Ford, I guess I don't need to ask you if you think it's unusual," Hereford baited.

"Nothing unusual so far. For you, this is pretty typical, really," Ford said evenly, temporarily containing his rage.

Ignoring the barb, Hereford turned his attention to Vanessa, who was still stunned. "My dear, at our current stakes, this hand was worth $3,600. I would love for you to join me for dinner tonight—your treat, of course."

The sound beating she was taking finally sunk in through the shock. Vanessa shot up from the table, clenched her fists, and stared down at Ford. Ford stood up, looked down at Vanessa, and said with a quiet ferocity, "Do not say one word to me." He walked out of the room to get a soda.

In a landmark event, Vanessa had been speechless through an entire hand.

Hereford was feeling his oats. He got up and sauntered out to the coffee area, peacocking for everybody in the club, but mostly for Vanessa. Beating her after that earlier comment about his net worth was, indeed, a gratifying experience. He came back in, sat down and picked up his cards. Ford opened four spades, and Hereford, having misheard, tried to overcall *two* hearts. Ford turned to Hereford and asked, "What did you bid?" Hereford seized the moment. Voice filled with disdain he sneered, "Two hearts. Two red, round, fat, fluffy, juicy hearts."

"Just checking. That's what I thought you bid," Ford said.

"Then why did you ask me?" Hereford snarled.

"Director!" Ford waited calmly. Penny rushed in.

"Yes?"

"We have a problem with the auction," Ford said.

"Problem? There's no problem with my two-heart bid." Hereford blustered.

"The auction went four spades by me, and my left-hand opponent bid, and I quote, 'Two red, round, fat, fluffy, juicy, hearts,'" Ford said smugly.

"You are a worthless ass, you know that?" Hereford said bitingly.

"Thank you. I have achieved my life's ambition. Worthlessness is hard to come by in this company; I mean with you being worth a fat, juicy two-heart bid," Ford deadpanned.

Hereford bit down hard on his anger, causing the thick vein in his forehead to throb purple under his deep tan.

Penny surveyed the table skeptically. They're all at it again, she thought to herself. "The ruling is that Vanessa can accept the two-heart bid. If she chooses not to, Hereford can make his bid sufficient and bid five hearts. If he does so, there are no penalties and the auction proceeds normally. If he does anything else, his partner is barred from the auction and there may be opening-lead penalties. Is that all for now?" she chastised their silliness with raised eyebrows.

"Thank you director," Ford said pleased with the course of events. "Shall we continue?" Ford felt the makings of a comeback. Not only did he and Vanessa end up with a good result on this deal, they had had no misunderstandings for the entire rubber.

The temporary turn of events had silenced Hereford and Parson; the room was hushed except for the occassional tip-tap of Vanessa's fingernail on the table top. Ford shuffled and Vanessa dealt. Ford shuffled optimistically, hoping to take the next couple of deals, get his client back to even on the match, and call it a day. But once he picked up his hand, concern flickered, sending doubt scurrying through his mind.

Vul: Both
Dlr: East

HEREFORD
♠ K Q 6 2
♡ A K Q
◇ J 10
♣ 10 7 5 2

FORD
♠ 7
♡ 10 6 5 3 2
◇ 6 5 2
♣ K 9 8 3

VANESSA
♠ J 10 9 8 4
♡ J 9 7
◇ 7 3
♣ A J 6

PARSON
♠ A 5 3
♡ 8 4
◇ A K Q 9 8 4
♣ Q 4

In his brief tenure as Vanessa's partner, Ford had learned to worry when he had a dearth of high cards. He often asked himself if it were worse for his opponents to have all the points, or his partner. Amazingly, the answer never seemed to get any clearer. Parson's vista was far more expansive. They were still comfortably ahead, though Hereford's lapse of concentration had not helped them any. Hereford didn't need to win every hand though; he was quite content with soundly beating his opponents overall. So far, they were still definitely on pace for that. Parson needed just one or two nice fat hands, and he would be on his way to collecting his 30% of the spoils. The important thing now was to prevent Hereford from doing anything ridiculous or getting into trouble with conventional misunderstandings.

Vanessa passed, and Parson considered his hand carefully. Typically, he would open with a strong no-trump, but he thought better of it and bid one diamond. Hereford responded with one spade, and they were off and running. Parson had to watch it now. It was crucial that Hereford did not get left in the dust of confusion, so Parson paused deliberately before bidding two diamonds. Ford looked up and stared right at Parson. But Parson was made of wood so old and so tough, he could not be felled by accusing eyes. His job was to win this hand by whatever means necessary, and nothing short of a court order was going to stop him from doing that. Slowness in the Hereford-Parson system was particularly designed to protect and support Hereford's penchant for overbidding; it showed—unabashedly—extra values.

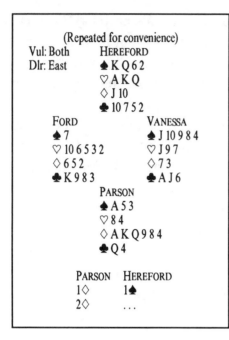

(Repeated for convenience)

Vul: Both   HEREFORD
Dlr: East   ♠ K Q 6 2
             ♡ A K Q
             ◇ J 10
             ♣ 10 7 5 2

FORD   VANESSA
♠ 7   ♠ J 10 9 8 4
♡ 10 6 5 3 2   ♡ J 9 7
◇ 6 5 2   ◇ 7 3
♣ K 9 8 3   ♣ A J 6

             PARSON
             ♠ A 5 3
             ♡ 8 4
             ◇ A K Q 9 8 4
             ♣ Q 4

PARSON   HEREFORD
1◇   1♠
2◇   . . .

Not only had Hereford become accustomed to tempo changes, he expected and relied on them. After Parson's slow two diamonds, Hereford's heart raced with exhilaration: he would finally get to use his new favorite convention. It was called "Roman Keycard Kickback," and it allowed a jump to the four level in the suit above trumps to ask about aces and the trump king. It was a simple modification of Blackwood, but it had great advantage over regular Blackwood in that it kept the bidding lower.

Armed with his splendid new convention, Hereford marched into battle and gloriously bid four hearts. He looked across to Parson as if to announce his triumph. Unfortunately, the look on Parson's face was anything but triumphant. His normally pale visage was even paler, and for someone already beyond the pale, this was quite an accomplishment. Parson began to mop his brow area with the slightly worn kerchief which he stowed in his pocket. He kept it there for trying times like these when Hereford decided to venture onto the four level, with nothing more than a memory of a convention that they had discussed one night, drunk.

Hereford waited for the alert. He had been accused many times of forgetting or butchering a convention, and as such, Hereford was fully aware that Parson did not have the proper amount of respect for his game. So he continued to wait patiently, trying to make eye contact with his partner.

Parson, meanwhile, was experiencing something that could be loosely described as night sweats here in the freezing, late afternoon. It was always a crap shoot as to whether Hereford remembered the convention or was just winging it. Complicating the matter was the tiny problem that the new alert rules no longer required an alert for this bid, but Hereford's pause indicated that he had not bothered to be up on the rules. Parson knew that if he didn't alert the bid, Hereford would be dangerously confused. Hereford might think that they were about to play in four hearts. Of course, there was always the chance he might actually know that Parson was about to respond to the request for keycards. Then again, Hereford could be thinking about anything, including what to have for dinner that night.

Precarious. There was simply no choice. Parson dug his left heel into the leg of the chair, squeezed his large buttocks tightly together, and did what had to be done. "Alert!" he gasped out as innocuously as he could.

"I can't believe this," Ford snarled, knowing Parson had just violated the alert rules. "This is beyond absurd."

Relieved, Hereford exhaled with half a laugh, "I was wondering what took you so long, partner."

"Oh, he just wanted to stay in tempo," Ford snapped, thoroughly disgusted. "Thank God you didn't deviate from the tempo of that slow two-diamond bid or I would have thought you were unethical. Since they were equally slow, I just assumed that you have never played a hand in under twenty minutes. Must be hell playing with all those time penalties." Ford's fiery eyes locked onto Hereford's, which were almost the same shade of pale blue as his own.

"Excuse me, are you questioning my partner's ethics?" Hereford drew on his ever-ready and seemingly inexhaustible supply of righteous indignation.

"Not just his, yours, too. Was that a confirmation bid when you chuckled about him taking so long to alert? You might as well have just stood up and announced, 'Yes, Parson, you have taken my bid the way I intended it.'"

Vanessa was far from clear on what exactly had happened. To her, Roman Keycard Kickback sounded less like a convention than a dance you engage in after consuming quite a number of gimlets. Murkily confused, she asked, "What does four hearts mean, exactly?"

"Don't even think of answering that, Parson," Ford jumped right back in the middle of things. "Vanessa," he continued, upbraiding her slightly, "why do you need to know that? Are you going to get into the auction here at the four level?" Ford was very frustrated, and he was taking control.

Vanessa gathered herself. She did not like being spoken to that way at all. She drew herself up haughtily and said, "I am entitled to know what their bid means, am I not?"

"Yes you are. But since you are not participating in this auction, there is no point in allowing them to clarify their methods to each other," Ford was firm. He had bigger, uglier fish to fry. Vanessa puffed angrily on the other side of the table. Parson's was a job well done, though; he and Hereford now had a perfect understanding of what was going on. Parson responded with four spades showing three keycards (in this case, two aces and the king of trumps). Realizing the hopelessness of the seven level, Hereford was content to bury his opponents in "only" six diamonds.

Vul: Both
Dlr: East

HEREFORD
♠ K Q 6 2
♡ A K Q
♢ J 10
♣ 10 7 5 2

FORD
♠ 7
♡ 10 6 5 3 2
♢ 6 5 2
♣ K 9 8 3

VANESSA
♠ J 10 9 8 4
♡ J 9 7
♢ 7 3
♣ A J 6

PARSON
♠ A 5 3
♡ 8 4
♢ A K Q 9 8 4
♣ Q 4

PARSON	HEREFORD
1♢	1♠
2♢*	4♡**
4♠***	6♢
Pass	

* = slow
** = Roman Keycard Kickback
*** = three keycards

137

Ford refused to concede. His brain fired with the desire to ruin these slimeballs. Briefly he considered leading his singleton spade, but knowing Hereford like the back of his hand, he decided there was a good chance that two club tricks might cash. Inexperienced players often bid Blackwood without controlling all four suits. He quickly dug out the club lead that would beat the contract.

The club three was led, the dummy hit, and Parson gave a robust "Well bid, partner!" Hereford sauntered around the table to look at Parson's hand. Hereford saw that they were off the first two club tricks, and that after Ford's accurate lead the slam was doomed. He patted Parson's thick shoulder and said, smiling, "These new conventions you're teaching me have brought our game to a new level." Parson played a low club from dummy and Vanessa took her ace, which left her looking at:

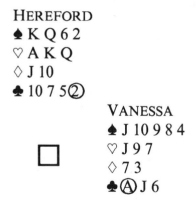

HEREFORD
♠ K Q 6 2
♡ A K Q
◇ J 10
♣ 10 7 5②

VANESSA
♠ J 10 9 8 4
♡ J 9 7
◇ 7 3
♣ Ⓐ J 6

□

Parson smoothly dropped the club queen, and with a Cheshire cat smile, he hungrily hovered at the edge of the table. To Vanessa, it seemed he was ready to spread his hand and claim. Beguiled by their confidence, she couldn't imagine any more top losers. There was simply no hope unless her partner somehow had a spade void, she reasoned, so she tabled the spade jack, causing Ford a somewhat unpleasant grinding sensation in his gut. Like indigestion, after eating too much shrapnel. He watched Parson scoop up this trick with relish, draw trumps, throw his other club loser on dummy's hearts and wrap up the slam.

Ford's head was spinning. He had made a great lead. They should have beaten the contract and been one step closer to evening the match. The singleton spade lead would have been a disaster; they would have had twelve easy tricks. He had found the club lead, but instead of a great result, he would probably have to listen to a great tirade from his boss.

Later, in the wee hours of the night, Ford went over the hands with Meyer. By then, Ford had lost his anger and most of his frustration. He was still baffled, though; he just couldn't understand how she could let herself be taken in by such a transparent con job. Why does she rely on her imaginary intuition instead of using good solid bridge logic. After winning the ace, she should know that declarer has another club, and probably not the king. From four small cards their partnership agreement had been to lead the second highest. Ford had led the three, indicating an honor. It had to be the king—she could see all the other honors. Declarer had to have another club because Ford couldn't have five. From five-card suits they led fourth-best . . . at least that's what the agreement was supposed to be. But then she never did bother to discuss or know their agreements.

Sitting at the table, in the stale, frigid air of the bridge club, Ford tried for a moment to contain himself. No, it was just too much for his heart to take. They should have beaten the scums' slam. Now Vanessa was losing some insane amount of money, and Ford was losing his peace of mind. Sanity at stake, Ford broke his personal code and questioned his partner, "Vanessa, why did you play the spade jack and not return a club?"

"Well, table feel, of course," she replied matter-of-factly. Evidently she hadn't yet realized they could have beaten the slam.

"Table feel? What exactly do you mean by table feel?" In his frustration, the question sounded more like an indictment.

"Mr. Maddox, I will not—," the Contessa began.

"No, Vanessa, what do you mean by table feel?" he insisted.

"I mean, Ford, that Parson said 'Well bid,' and they were both very, very confident," she defended.

"Confident? They were lying. They used the lying to cheat, and the cheating to steal. Stealing from you. That hand was worth $3,000 and brings our total losses on the day to somewhere around $6,000."

Hereford jumped in: "It doesn't surprise me in the least that you are trying to lay this off on us. Vanessa, this is what second-rate pros do. They can't get the job done, so they blame somebody else. Maddox is probably afraid of you, or he'd blame you. He's blaming us instead, insulting our ethics," Hereford cavalierly proclaimed, confident in the obviousness of this truth.

"Yeah, right. Even with all of your hesitations, false alerts, and acting job, the club lead combined with a club return, not the spade jack, still beats the hand. Look at the cards. Seriously, Vanessa, you should call the police. You have been robbed." Ford did not give an inch. He was disgusted.

"So, you *are* calling me a cheater, aren't you, Maddox? You just don't have the guts to look me in the eyes and say it." Hereford's vein was throbbing again.

"To tell you the absolute truth, Hereford," Ford said calmly, looking earnestly into Hereford's eyes, "if you spent half—just half—of the time you spend working out your cheating methods working on your bridge, you wouldn't be such a bad player. You probably wouldn't have to hire anyone. Of course, your pro won't tell you that. He wants you to be dependent on these little wormy ways. He wants you to wait for the illegal alert, to rely on the slow bid."

Parson, with the thick skin of the cockroach, collected the cards and began to shuffle. He thought nothing of it. To him, it was all part of the game.

For Hereford, too, it was all part of the game. But a much different game that had very little to do with bridge. Currently, he was losing. Rather badly, in fact. Outraged, Hereford shouted venomously at Ford, "Work on my bridge?" Losing all control, he continued ferociously, "What, like you? You've done absolutely nothing with your life. Wasted it, threw it away playing cards all the time. You are thirty-something years old, and you are still working for someone else. When I was thirty, I was building my empire. But no, that wasn't good enough for you, that money was dirty, that business was bad. So, my son, my very own flesh and blood, will spend the rest of his living days wasting his mind and moving from job to job. You are no longer my son. You are a damn disgrace! I will leave you nothing, and if you starve to death in your old age, it's your choice. You don't have the common sense God gave a cow! You are no longer a Willis. You will be penniless." Hereford's face was pale and moist; he looked as if he had narrowly avoided a coronary.

Vanessa looked up, in utter disbelief. *"Your son? But you don't even have the same last name*!?" she questioned the table. Receiving no response, she turned to Parson. *"Well?"* she puzzled.

Parson whispered, "Ford took his mother's name. Not many people know the story."

Ford's face flamed red. He shot the words out of his mouth, bullets of truth, aimed at the heart: "Penniless? Maybe, but not nameless. I am a Maddox. You are the one who has lost his name. You have sold it, given it away, really. You spent your good name cheating for petty victories. You'd sell your morals—if you had any left. What, Hereford, you think people don't know how unethical you are? Why do you think I don't use your name? Winning a game of cards is important enough to cheat? What's the point? So you can lie to yourself and tell yourself you really are good, because you know you would not have won that hand, any hand, without cheating. If winning was honestly that important to you, you would work for it. You would bust your butt to learn and practice and discipline your desire to win. But it's not about winning for you; it's about beating someone else. It's about power. You want them all to be talking about you at the club, any club. You would rather screw someone else over at the table than win, because then you have the power. But, you're still a lousy card player at the end of the match. And you'll still be a lousy human being at the end of your life. And all your pennies can't buy you a name for that empty space on your marble headstone, get it?"

"No son of mine. You are a bastard." Hereford's bitter words cracked in the cold, air-conditioned room.

"You wish I was. I am your son. I am the man you never had the heart to be," Ford replied coldly. With that, he folded his hands in his lap and sat back.

Hereford turned his eyes and snatched his keys from the side table. He stalked out of the room dragging his rage behind him.

Parson had been holding the deck of cards so long in his hand, he had trouble setting them down on the table. He seemed slightly shaken. Standing up, he looked at Ford and said, "Thank you, Ford." Shrouded in mystery, Parson disappeared.

Ford and Vanessa looked at each other, baffled.

"Well, Vanessa, sorry we lost," Ford conciliated.

"Are you okay, Ford?" Vanessa's concerned voice surprised him.

"Oh, yeah. That's my father. Listen, there's a couple of things we should go over tomorrow. We'll practice and then challenge them to a rematch. We'll beat 'em."

"You would actually play him again?" Vanessa stared in disbelief.

"As long as he plays bridge, I will play him again," Ford said smoothly.

Ebb & Flow

Ford sat bemused in the passenger seat as Meyer guided the faded black Olds '98 smoothly into the strip-mall parking lot. "This thing handles pretty well for a boat. Of course, you need a couple of nautical miles to turn around in, but hey, you're the captain of your own destiny," Ford taunted.

"It's Admiral to you buddy," Meyer retorted, and pulled up next to Penny's car.

"So what's your guess as to why we're here?" Ford asked curiously.

"Hmm. Don't know. Surprise birthday party for me is one possibility," Meyer said.

"Yeah, but Richie'd be here. His car's gone." Ford refused Meyer the satisfaction of a chuckle. They got out of the air-conditioned car and were swallowed up by the Miami heat. As they walked toward Richie's bridge club, Ford watched a young, carrot-topped boy dash across the black lava asphalt, barefoot. "Where are that kid's shoes?" he wondered out loud.

"Huh?" Meyer had not seen it.

"Nothing," Ford said with a head shake.

Ford followed Meyer through the heavy glass door. The burdensome heat outside was nothing less than stifling inside. Meyer looked at Penny, who was scrubbing, and soaking wet. "Is the air conditioning broken, or is it set on 90?"

"The landlord pays the utilities," she said, wiping her sweaty forehead with her sticky arm.

145

"And . . . ?" Meyer didn't think that answer was particularly explanatory.

"And, Richie hasn't paid the landlord," she said, thinking the whole matter was all rather obvious.

"Hey, but it's a nice change from Vanessa's," Ford said. "Just don't serve egg salad."

"The rate we're going, we're not going to be serving anything," Penny nipped.

Ignoring Penny's bad mood, Meyer grinningly asked Ford, "Did you notice she said, 'We're'?"

"That's why they pay you the big bucks, Admiral," Ford snickered, "for noticing all those clues."

"Okay, okay," Penny sighed, "I said, 'we're.' Richie asked me if I would help him get things together here. You know . . . and I said yes, of course. So let's not make much ado about nothing; we're working together. That's why I called you guys to come over."

"Look, I'm happy to work, but we've got to get a good fan or something," Meyer said, studying the small, sputtering thing she had. It looked like a watch with egg beaters attached. Small egg beaters.

"No, I don't want you to work—at least not today. What we need are some ideas, a plan." Penny's determination permeated the heat.

"All right," Meyer said seriously, "Plan for what, exactly?"

Bewildered by his question, she prodded his brain, "For the club, Meyer."

"Oh yeah. Look," Meyer said as the sweat trickled down the side of his neck, "I'm just half a step slower when it's 1,000 degrees in the room, okay?"

146

Penny ignored him; she was onto the next thought. "The way I see it, all it really needs is some cosmetic work. Like ripping off this gross wallpaper, painting, maybe adding a little molding around the ceiling. Same for the bathroom," excitement flashed in her voice, "a new sink, some paint, flowers maybe, some new floor tile. Just small stuff like that; it will make a huge difference. Management-wise, we could restructure the way the bridge classes are held, get some guest speakers, host sectionals; the clients will come back, I'm sure of it. That's all Vanessa did—"

"Whoa, wait a minute," Ford interrupted. "If Richie can't pay the landlord, how's he gonna pay for all that?"

"That's where the plan comes in," Penny said, her eyes glimmering.

"Let me guess. You're thinking a Brinks truck? Or maybe dabbling in the gun-running business?" Ford was skeptical. If it were that easy to come up with money, everybody'd be doing it.

"I've got to sit down. It's too hot to think standing up," Meyer said.

"Okay, there's a table set up way in the back, over there." Penny pointed the way.

"Let's start this from the beginning," Meyer said.

"Beginning? Meyer, I'll never make it," Ford protested. "What beginning are you talking about?"

"The beginning of how Richie got into this predicament," Meyer insisted.

"I can answer that and save all the time of analyzing this to death, because even if I had the patience, which I don't, I do have to work today," Ford said.

"Meyer, Richie lost a couple of bets. He got a little behind, made another couple of bets, and lost again. Vanessa opened her club, right time, right place, badda-bing, badda-boom, he's in the soup."

Meyer gave Ford *The Look*.

"Okay, for Chrissake, Penny, what happened?" Ford asked, guilt-trodden.

"Vanessa happened, and in a big way. She stole the clients, and his business is really struggling. It's getting to him. It really is." Penny's disheartened eyes dropped to her lap.

"Where is he now?" Meyer asked.

"He's with the landlord trying to work something out," she answered slowly.

"Chin up, Pen. We have the man with the plan with us. We'll come up with something," Ford rallied.

Meyer talked to himself, thinking out loud, "We need money, but we can't borrow it; we need to get back the clients who left, hmm . . . mmm. A charity event. That's it," he proclaimed.

"Charity? Richie'll never go for it," Penny said, rejecting the idea.

"Wait. We run a bridge event. Ford and I will play with everyone who attends and pays a fee. The fee goes toward the club renovation. Let us show you how to renovate your old game, or something like that. A theme thing." Meyer loved this idea.

"But we can't get enough money in one session." Penny's pessimism prevailed.

"Two-day event. Everyone gets to play. Weekend with Ford and Meyer . . . or whatever," Ford chimed in.

Penny ran through the idea a couple of times in her head. "Yes, yes. Yes, I think it just might work, guys. We can promote this all over the area. We'll even hit the adjacent areas, I mean, you two are big enough names to draw people from all over. We'll hang some big tarps up with signs that say 'Renovation in progress,' and we'll give that other club a run . . . "

"*Give that other club what, you treasonous little tramp,*" a voice yowled from behind them. Ford knew that yowl well. It was the unearthly sound Vanessa made right before her head spun around like Satan's Bride. His neck spasmed.

"I knew you were up to something when you wanted to come in late today. I figured you were chasing around after some man. God knows you have no sense, to fall all over for some has-been bridge club run by some never-was bridge player. You could have had a career with me," Vanessa chastised.

"A career?" Penny shot back sarcastically. "Doing what? Making coffee? Babysitting you and Hereford? Arranging the cookies so they look like flowers? Boy, that's an offer I can hardly turn down."

Meyer had never seen Penny so angry.

"A person in your position should have considered it. Too late. I will send your things with Mr. Maddox, who will be unable to attend this little shindig of yours or he will find himself like you—sitting in a rathole plotting for cheese. You are fired." The Contessa planted her heels, whirled like a dervish (a maneuver that, frankly, still amazed Ford every time he saw it), and vanished into the heavy heat.

"Where did she come from?" Ford was more than a little undone. His client had found her way into his private life. This did not bode well.

"It wasn't Eden; I'll tell you that," Meyer gasped in disbelief. "She must have spotted Penny's car in the parking lot."

"Oh yeah, she has to drive by here to get to her club." Ford focused his consoling eyes on Penny. "Hey, I'm really sorry you got fired."

"Don't be sorry about that job. Working for a petty tyrant is not how I want to spend my life. I'm not sorry in the least. Richie and I are going to make this work, I'm confident," she spoke resolutely. "I feel worse for you, Ford. *You* have to go back."

"Today, in fact. Pretty soon. I have to go back soon," Ford cleared his throat. "Damn." Doubt shadowed Ford's eyes.

"Speaking of which, what about our business plan?" Penny said, with a general's pragmatism. "It was contingent on your being able to play, Ford." She met his eyes.

"Let me worry about that. You guys set up the rest. I'll be here," Ford said reassuringly, but it was hard to tell if he was promising her or himself. "But I could live without stripping wallpaper," Ford said, laughing too loudly. Meyer stared hard at his friend. He had known Ford long enough to know: Ford was worried.

* * * * * * * * *

Parson sank sullenly into his faded couch. At this moment, each lump in the seat cushion was particularly offensive to his body; he had been besieged by a vile headache, of the migraine variety. He stared through the dimness to the shelves that lined the room. He really needed to dust, and to rearrange some of his collections. He wanted to feature his colorful mount of fly-fishing flies behind the chair Mother always sat in. As her name entered his awareness, he felt a sharp pain just behind his right eye; the migraine had taken a turn for the worse. He reached over the arm of the couch and yanked the lamp plug out of the wall, extinguishing the only light in the room. The apartment settled into darkness, reverberating with the hum of the air conditioner. He gingerly laid his head on the couch pillow and hoped sleep would take him soon. Parson's failure to access the deal generator weighed heavily on his mind. Very likely this would cost him his job. Worse yet, Hereford might continue to pay him—less, of course—and simply humiliate him daily. Multiply that by the Mother Grief Factor, which made any difficult situation exponentially more painful, and he found himself lying like a beached whale on a lumpy couch in a dark apartment with a raging migraine. He tucked his hands beneath his chin and let his white belly flop over the edge of the couch. Sleep. Slee-ee-eep.

The first ring of the phone ripped through his head like a meteor. Desperate for sleep, he tried to ignore it. But each ring sent pain flashing into his brain, blinding him from the inside out. He sent a listless hand to pick up the receiver.

"Hello," he answered in the hushed tones of an undertaker.

"Parson," the voice tolled through the line, "how are you?"

The next to last person on earth I want to talk to, Parson thought pitifully. "Not well, Hereford, not well at all. What can I do for you?" Parson asked abruptly. There would be no dallying on the phone if he could help it.

"I'm calling, my dear boy, to check on the status of our Plan. What is the progress report? Where do we stand?" Hereford inquired.

"The progress report is a blank sheet of paper. We have made no progress, not a scrap, not an inch, not one lick. Nothing at all. That's where we stand," Parson said plainly. He was too weak to be anything other than forthright.

"Hopelessness never solved a problem. Nothing is hopeless, period," Hereford emphasized. "Every problem can be solved, every system can be beaten, given the right resources. We have those resources. Brains, money, and willpower. So what is the difficulty?" Hereford interrogated.

The pain of Parson's blinding migraine made him somewhat belligerent. "We can't access the League's deal generator. That's the problem. Same one as it was before," he added peevishly.

"And the girl, Jenny?" Hereford pressed.

"*Penny*, Hereford, it's *Penny*. I spoke with Penny. She was zero help. She doesn't have the faintest idea how to access the computer."

"I thought she had the code?" Hereford dogged.

"Yes, when she worked there she did. But they change the code frequently, and she doesn't know the algorithm that generates it. I have personally spent hours trying to figure it out, but it has been utterly fruitless. If anything, I am worse off than I was." Parson's petulant voice grated on Hereford.

"Do you think she was on to you?" Hereford pursued the next possibility.

"What?" Parson started in disbelief.

"Parson, do you think she knew that you were trying to get information out of her?" he clarified.

"Ridiculous, Hereford. Absolutely not. She had no idea. She clearly likes me," Parson asserted.

"Truth is stranger than fiction, eh? Okay, let's think again." Hereford would not be defeated.

"Look, maybe we can try communicating by some sort of method . . ." Parson suggested.

"You are referring to the Pencil Precision scandal, where the people used writing utensils? I think not." Hereford bridled at the thought. "First of all, the League would spy that immediately. It's been done. Secondly— and most importantly—it was unsuccessful. That's why we know about it, right?" Hereford's patience had hopped a bus out of town. Parson's stupidity was maddening.

"Well, in the end it failed, yes. But during the interim it was obviously very successful. We only need it for one tournament," Parson defended.

"No, that is a horrible idea. The method must be comprehensive and untraceable. It must be flawless. If we are disciplined and tenacious, we can beat this system. We can be the greatest pair in the country. Achieving the perfect deception is an art form."

Christ, thought Parson, this guy is too much. Why doesn't he just learn to play better; all that crap about discipline and hard work. Please. He held his thoughts and continued, "Yes, well, perfect art, like perfect anything, exists in theory only, Hereford. There's no way to do this without significant risk. There is no perfect cheating scheme."

"Your vision is limited by your practicality, my boy. It inhibits your creativity. Create a better mousetrap, catch more mice. No need to worry about losing the cheese."

"Not at all, Hereford. Practicality hones my creativity. This ideal scheme of yours doesn't exist. Humans aren't perfect, and anything they design is not perfect. Besides, the only thing approaching perfection is knowing the hands. No way to know the hands if we can't generate them," Parson said reasonably.

Hereford dug in. He hated this defeatist mentality. "I'll make you a wager. If I can figure out a way to win—which, incidentally, was your job—you keep your job for the next year with no salary increase. And, at the regional tournaments, I pay only for your expenses, no salary. What do you say?"

"And if you can't figure out a way to win?" Parson considered.

"Double your current salary," Hereford said confidently.

Parson paused. He started to reply, changed his mind, and kept perfectly still. With Hereford, the stakes were never what they seemed. If Hereford won, every paycheck he wrote would be accompanied by gloating and humiliation. Hereford played for dignity, pride, and self-respect, and Parson wasn't up for wagering that.

"Is something the matter, my dear Parson?" Hereford's chastising inflections tore into Parson's ego. "Silence, eh? Cat got your tongue?" Hereford smirked, knowing that Parson was squirming in Failure's snare. He had failed to be sure, but Parson's hardened shell of practicality protected him from the temptation of Hereford's baiting. Though seared by the fire of humiliation, Parson was no fool. No, if Hereford was ready to bet, odds were that he already had a plan. Or, he would make one, simply in spite of Parson, just to show he could. Hereford had a will like that. Very spiteful and determined.

"No, I'm declining that bet, Hereford," Parson finally answered. "I have complete confidence in your abilities in these matters," he said equitably.

"Harumpf," Hereford grumped. "Wish I could say the same of you. It doesn't seem to remotely bother you that you have utterly failed to complete this task, hmm, Parson?" Hereford attacked.

Parson winced painfully on the other end of the phone. "Hereford," he steeled his voice, "it doesn't bother me in the least. Not remotely."

"Well, I suppose that shouldn't surprise me. Never send a boy to do a man's job, they say. I'll be in touch," Hereford concluded. "Oh, Parson?" Hereford sang out one last barb.

"Yes, Hereford," Parson said, obviously bored.

"In case you were wondering, after we win, you're fired," and with that, Hereford sent the receiver sailing into the cradle that stood on his desk, walked across the expanse of his office and opened the large door to yell at his secretary publicly. She never knew her good fortune, for she was down the hall, collating copies. "Damn," he cursed, kicking his socked foot futilely in the air.

"Aargh," he growled, and slammed the heavy door as best he could.

Parson hung up the empty phone unaffected. He was no longer a failing member of Hereford's muddled cabal. Once freed from Hereford's ruthless dominion, Parson eagerly anticipated burrowing his way into a sweeter, richer fruit. The Contessa was an apple almost ripe for the picking. He hopped up off the couch and trotted into the kitchen. To his delight, his headache had magically disappeared and he believed he had three of yesterday's chocolate glazed doughnuts stashed in the bottom drawer next to the sink awaiting just such a moment. He unboxed the doughnuts, placed them on a paper towel and poured a glass of tomato juice. His mind explored job possibilities. He predicted there was a good chance Vanessa would be available as a client. Ford Maddox would not be able to take much more of that, Parson assessed; too thin-skinned. Never did understand how that guy stayed in business, Parson thought, and happily bit into his second doughnut.

The Queen's Court

On the ride to work Ford began bracing himself for the big scene. Combine Vanessa's acting penchant with the lovely scene at Richie's they had just had, add the audience of patrons at Vanessa's club, stir, and bake at 350 degrees of Vanessa's rage. Voilà! A beautiful Oscar-winning performance by Vanessa, frosted with his role of Best Supporting Actor . . . *And I would like to thank my friend Penny for getting me this job, my friend Meyer for saying I told you so at least a million times, and of course, Vanessa, without whom I could have never had such a miserable existence* . . . At least I haven't lost my perspective, Ford thought to himself as he turned into the parking lot surrounding Trumps.

He walked into the club, resigned to being an unwilling participant in yet another one of the Contessa's dramas. He wondered how Parson could do this, month after month, year after year; Hereford, after all, had his own particularly awful brand of scene-making. Vanessa stood stiffly atop her spiked-heels and chatted with a patron. As Ford approached, she fixed her eyes on him, flipped him a cursory smile, and checked her watch. He was early. Not recognizing the patron, Ford smiled and warmly extended his goodwill, "Hi, I'm Ford Maddox." The conversation dwindled quickly, and the patron hungrily made her way to the luncheon buffet, leaving Ford and Vanessa standing alone.

Ford noticed a clammy feeling climbing over his entire body. The Contessa primly turned to face him. He tensed. Quietly articulating each word, she said, "Penny's things are in the coat closet by the front door. Please take them when you leave."

Ford said nothing, waiting for the other lemon-yellow, spike-heeled Miami sandal to drop.

"Mr. Maddox?" She toyed with his name in the frigid atmosphere of the air-conditioned room. "Did you hear me?" she asked with just the slightest edge in her voice.

"Uh, excuse me, yes, of course, right. I'll get the stuff when I go," Ford stumbled.

"You thought I was going to yell, I presume?" She pulled a sinister smile across her tight facial skin.

But far from being lulled by her calmness, Ford was wary. "Yell about what?" he countered evenly.

"Some employers would be angry upon discovering their employees were plotting to put them out of business," she spoke slowly.

Ford's sea-blue eyes did not move from hers. He stood calmly, refusing to bend under the weight of her insinuation. The challenge of his silence forced her hand.

"Playing in a bridge game designed to put me out of business could fairly be called a breach of contract," she continued.

"Maybe, maybe not," he said, addressing her thinly-veiled threat. "In any case, that hasn't happened," he concluded.

"No, *that* hasn't happened. And, I am quite confident that *it* won't," her smile had dissolved into a grimace. She collected her pencil and convention card from a nearby table and steamed off to Table One, their usual starting position. I despise being threatened, thought Ford, disgusted with his situation. But, he congratulated himself, I knew the real Vanessa was in there somewhere.

Ford had a few minutes until game time, so he cruised over to the luncheon table. The one good thing about playing in Vanessa's club was the food. It was always fresh, interesting, and delicious. (It was too cold for anything to spoil. Even milk and butter were safe unrefrigerated for weeks.) The waitress approached him and asked if she could fix him a plate, but he declined. Making the food choices was half the fun. He overheard Maura explaining, in rather graphic detail, the detrimental effects of food like this. The recipient of this advice was, perhaps, the *most* unwilling listener in the room, Eileen Gready. Ford appreciated Eileen; they each had a voracious appetite, although she seemed to absorb both his and her calories.

"Hey there, Eileen. What looks good today?" he enthusiastically asked, gesturing to the spread on the table.

"Oh, Ford. Nice to see you," her deep voice rumbled up from her belly. "I'll tell you, sweetie, that Vanessa sure knows how to feed people. Doesn't treat them so well, but you can overlook some things for good food," she laughed and threw Ford a wink. Ford joined her laughter and patted her shoulder. She was right. They fixed their plates together, joking and sampling as they went.

"Okay, Eileen, it's show time," Ford said merrily. He enjoyed her.

"Yes, I guess it *is* show time for you." She gave a knowing smile and a gentle, teasing shove to Ford's arm. "Enjoy yourself as best you can. See you later." Balancing two plates and a large drink, Eileen lumbered off cheerfully to play.

Ford headed for his table. He set his food down,

seated himself, and proceeded to have yet another unbelievably difficult day with the charming Contessa.

Eileen sat down heavily in the plush North chair several tables away. She never sat East-West; moving from table to table was too much exercise. She was the last one to join the foursome. Her partner, Gilda, did not mind though; she had been entertaining (or boring, depending on how you looked at it) the opponents with stories of her son's most recent successes, her daughter's most recent acquisitions, and her grandchildren's most recent grades. Prissy, who usually had a pronounced aversion to Eileen, especially around feeding time, gave Eileen the warmest, friendliest welcome to the table. She was determined to thoroughly enjoy one of her last club games with Maura before the nationals in Chicago. "Eileen, so glad to see you today," she gushed.

"If you've been sitting here long with Gilda, I'll bet you are," Eileen chuckled at her own honesty. Gilda was a good partner, but those stories could wear on your nerves after a while. "Okay gals, let's play. As Ford just said to me, 'It's show time!'" Eileen belted out.

"That Ford is sweet, isn't he?" Maura said.

"Absolutely, darling," Gilda beamed.

As the foursome drew their cards from the board, they heard quite a commotion at the next table. The patrons were having a heated discussion over the grave issue of whether to have *both* boards on the table, or just one at a time. "I guess," Eileen said loudly, "they don't have anything else to worry about." And with that, she picked up the North cards and set her mind to playing bridge.

Vul: N-S
Dlr: West

EILEEN
♠ K J 7
♡ A J 8 4
◊ 6 2
♣ Q J 5 4

PRISCILLA
♠ 8 2
♡ Q 9 7 6 2
◊ 10 8 4 3
♣ 8 7

MAURA
♠ A Q 10 9
♡ 3
◊ A Q J 9 5
♣ K 9 2

GILDA
♠ 6 5 4 3
♡ K 10 5
◊ K 7
♣ A 10 6 3

WEST	NORTH	EAST	SOUTH
PRISCILLA	EILEEN	MAURA	GILDA
Pass	1♣	1◊	1♠
3◊*	Pass	Pass	Double
Pass	3♠	Pass	3NT
Pass	Pass	Double	Pass
Pass	4♡	Double	Pass
Pass	4♠	Double	All Pass

* = Weak

Between bites, Eileen opened a gruff one club. Without hesitation, Maura overcalled one diamond. Gilda bid her four-card major. Prissy, feeling dashing because she played the modern style, jumped to three diamonds showing a weak hand with four trumps. Quietness closed around the players. Prissy was titillated that her three-diamond bid caused such a hush. The auction came back around to Gilda, who found herself encumbered by

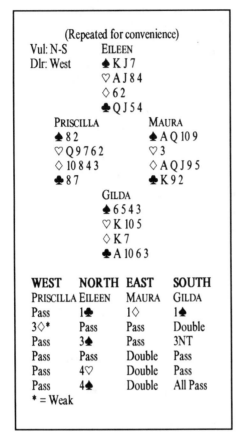

	(Repeated for convenience)		
Vul: N-S	EILEEN		
Dlr: West	♠ K J 7		
	♡ A J 8 4		
	◇ 6 2		
	♣ Q J 5 4		

PRISCILLA	MAURA
♠ 8 2	♠ A Q 10 9
♡ Q 9 7 6 2	♡ 3
◇ 10 8 4 3	◇ A Q J 9 5
♣ 8 7	♣ K 9 2

	GILDA
	♠ 6 5 4 3
	♡ K 10 5
	◇ K 7
	♣ A 10 6 3

WEST	NORTH	EAST	SOUTH
PRISCILLA	EILEEN	MAURA	GILDA
Pass	1♣	1◇	1♠
3◇*	Pass	Pass	Double
Pass	3♠	Pass	3NT
Pass	Pass	Double	Pass
Pass	4♡	Double	Pass
Pass	4♠	Double	All Pass
* = Weak			

indecision. She lingered for a few moments, and eventually doubled.

This hesitation was far more than Eileen could tolerate. Unaware of the potential ethical infraction of pulling a slow double, Eileen retreated to the illusionary safety of three spades. Things were moving along, Gilda thought; why not play in a notrump game instead of the potential 4-3 fit. Notrump might offer the same nine tricks, but a better payoff. Maybe, Gilda thought optimistically, the clubs would run for a source of tricks.

She bid three notrump, but upon hearing Maura's double, Eileen thought better of it and ran to four hearts. Maura, realizing her partner must have some heart length, doubled again. Even Maura's spirits rose from the dead when she got to double four spades.

Prissy led a club and Eileen sheepishly tabled her dummy. Gilda immediately realized they were in an awful contract. *Yis-gadal v'yis-kadash sh'mey rabah*, she murmured, shaking her head.

"What's she saying," Prissy asked Eileen.

"Kaddish, the Jewish prayer for the dead, honey. Prayer for the dead," Eileen said dejectedly.

Gilda played dummy's club queen, and it held the trick. Declarer, not thinking the preempter had the heart queen, tried a heart to her ten losing to West's queen. Priscilla continued with clubs to declarer's ten. Declarer, struggling, led a trump up. Low, jack, queen. Maura gave her partner a club ruff. Elated, Prissy exited with a diamond to Maura's ace. This was followed by another diamond that put declarer in hand, leaving:

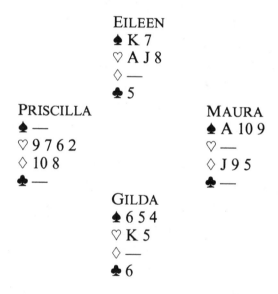

EILEEN
♠ K 7
♡ A J 8
♦ —
♣ 5

PRISCILLA
♠ —
♡ 9 7 6 2
♦ 10 8
♣ —

MAURA
♠ A 10 9
♡ —
♦ J 9 5
♣ —

GILDA
♠ 6 5 4
♡ K 5
♦ —
♣ 6

Declarer had already lost a heart, a diamond, a spade and a club ruff for at least down one. With some really good luck, maybe the spade ace would fall, and she could miraculously salvage down two. This thought was accompanied by her prayers. She tried another spade towards dummy, hoping . . . Prissy showed out and Gilda almost had a coronary. Steadfast, Maura won this trick, drew the trumps, and took the diamonds for the rest of the tricks. Down seven, a whopping 2,000.

Priscilla jotted down the score and looked up at her partner. "I think we might win again today, Maura." She began to see the headlines touting their huge win in Chicago. Gilda whipped her head around and glowered. Eileen snorted, disgruntled. She hated losing, and was tough on partners when she did.

"Gilda, Why on earth did you bid three notrump? Maura didn't double us in three spades," Eileen said. She bellowed to the waitress, "'Scuse me, hello? I want another Coke. Make sure it's regular, not diet. I hate diet."

"Forget about why I bid three notrump, Eileen. Obviously I thought we might make a game. I think the question is, and don't you agree with me, Maura honey, the question is why on earth did you pull?" Gilda was indignant at the attack. She tossed her shoulders back and pushed her chest forward. Who was Eileen to be talking to her that way? "In fact," Gilda renewed the battle, "I can make three notrump if I guess the hearts," she said decisively.

"If you say so," Eileen shrugged dismissively. "Hey, where's the ice?" she yelled out to the waitress. The waitress gestured, and Eileen looked down. "Oh, here it is. The problem is, Gilda, you didn't guess them in four spades doubled," Eileen paused to take a long drink of her Coke, "so I just don't see why you would guess hearts in three notrump." Her hard voice rode roughly over Gilda.

"Ladies," Maura interjected, "please don't argue. It's bad for your hearts, livers, and bladders."

"If I don't argue now, Eileen will use this against me later," Gilda complained.

Prissy let out an untimely laugh. "I was just thinking," she said, smoothing her hair, "about that couple that used to play here on Wednesday nights; I think it was Wednesdays. Maura, remember them?" she giggled self-consciously.

"Which couple, dear?" Maura looked strained.

"The man with that big handlebar mustache, and his little wife. He always yelled at her at the table. He would berate her really, all the time. She had lovely clothes, but, you know, I didn't think she had a very good haircut," Prissy lost herself in her memory.

"He was an unpleasant man with a ferocious temper," Maura agreed, "probably bilious."

"Back to my point, Eileen," Gilda said, annoyed, rapidly tapping her largest ring on the table top. "I did what I did because in spades I had entry problems. In three notrump, I'd be able to pick up the hearts and clubs at my leisure. Don't you see, they'd lead diamonds and I might lay down the heart king out of convenience," she was thoroughly agitated now. "Where'd that waitress go? All the chicken salad sandwiches are going to be gone. I think the help here is very poor. Vanessa should not have skimped on help," she soundly chastised Vanessa, to compensate for what she dared not say to her partner, if she wanted to continue playing bridge. "Anyway," Gilda offered one last nudge, "I think plus 750 would be better than minus 2,000."

"Can't we get on with this next hand," Eileen grunted as she pulled the North cards from the board.

Vul: None   EILEEN
Dlr: North   ♠ K Q 5 3
      ♡ —
      ◇ A J 8 7 6 2
      ♣ A 5 4

PRISCILLA   MAURA
♠ 8 7 4 2   ♠ J 10 9 6
♡ Q 10   ♡ A K J 2
◇ K Q 10 9 4   ◇ 5
♣ Q 7   ♣ J 10 8 3

      GILDA
      ♠ A
      ♡ 9 8 7 6 5 4 3
      ◇ 3
      ♣ K 9 6 2

WEST	NORTH	EAST	SOUTH
PRISCILLA	EILEEN	MAURA	GILDA
—	1◇	1♡	Pass
2◇	2♠	Pass	Pass
3♡	Pass	Pass	Double
All Pass			

Eileen studied her hand and opened the bidding
with one diamond. Maura, who had the perfect shape
for a takeout double, didn't think 10 high-card points
were enough for that action, so she made the reasonable
overcall of one-heart. She was glad she remembered
reading Mike Lawrence's advice to overcall on the one
level with a good four-card suit; it came in handy to keep
up with your bridge theory.

Maura's one-heart overcall left Gilda, with the
South cards, utterly baffled. How could Maura bid

hearts when Gilda had seven of them herself? Was this an artificial bid by Maura, Gilda wondered, slightly panicked. And how am I to show *my* seven hearts? Shoot, Gilda thought, a two-heart bid is not natural; it shows a good hand in support of diamonds.

Confused, Gilda turned to Prissy and asked, "What does one heart show?"

Prissy puckered her face and said sourly, "I imagine it means that *you* have hearts! If it was anything other than natural I would have alerted, wouldn't I?"

Gilda dawdled a little longer, anxiously tapping her largest gemstone against the tabletop. Her eyes darted between her hand and her partner, looking for some clue as to what to do. With a heavy sigh, she finally concluded all she could do was pass, which she did, rather theatrically.

Prissy drew herself up straight in the chair and pulled a scowl over her usually kind face. She sniffed and looked accusingly over her glasses. Looking at her own diamond suit, Prissy proudly beat back the desire to snidely ask what Eileen's one-diamond bid meant; although, Prissy noted to herself, that would certainly serve Gilda right. Caught up in the heat of things, Priscilla forgot herself and offered a naive 1950's two-diamond bid, hoping to show a natural hand. Heck, she had diamonds, why not bid them? But this was the 1990's, and Maura would interpret two diamonds as a cue-bid showing a good heart raise.

Slurping down her third Coke, Eileen bid two spades, introducing her side suit. Maura calmly passed, and the bidding fell to Gilda again. Tiny pearls of sweat were beginning to appear at her hairline. She had become thoroughly flustered; not only had her opponents bid her seven-card heart suit, but her partner was bidding suits in which she had only singletons. Exasperated, she started breathing in small, anxious huffs and squirming in her seat. Her partner, focused on getting the waitress's attention, was quite unaware of Gilda's discomfort until Gilda began shushing the table nearest them with so much zeal you would think she was campaigning for Congress. Eileen looked up and remarked, "Gilda, leave those poor players alone. They are not talking loudly. Just bid your hand, please."

At this point in the auction, Gilda clearly should have corrected to diamonds since that rated to be Eileen's longer suit. Strangely enough, the 4-1 spade fit would produce eight tricks unless the defense led a trump. In spades, declarer could take the ace of diamonds, the ace-king of clubs, a diamond ruff with dummy's singleton spade ace, two heart ruffs with the three and five of spades, and the king-queen of trumps. More out of fear than anything else, Gilda passed two spades and it was up to Prissy.

Priscilla had always been uncomfortable defending against two-level contracts, so she decided to avoid the problem altogether by bidding three hearts. So what if she had only two-card support; they were two good ones. Gilda brightened visibly. She was saved! This was nothing short of a miracle. "Eileen," she said excitedly, "order a Coke for me, too. And some food." She almost giggled. When three hearts came around to her, Gilda belted out a zesty "Double!"

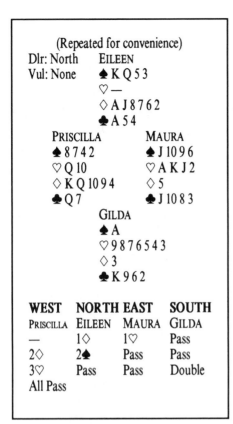

(Repeated for convenience)
Dlr: North   EILEEN
Vul: None   ♠ K Q 5 3
              ♡ —
              ◇ A J 8 7 6 2
              ♣ A 5 4

PRISCILLA   MAURA
♠ 8 7 4 2   ♠ J 10 9 6
♡ Q 10   ♡ A K J 2
◇ K Q 10 9 4   ◇ 5
♣ Q 7   ♣ J 10 8 3

              GILDA
              ♠ A
              ♡ 9 8 7 6 5 4 3
              ◇ 3
              ♣ K 9 6 2

WEST	NORTH	EAST	SOUTH
PRISCILLA	EILEEN	MAURA	GILDA
—	1◇	1♡	Pass
2◇	2♠	Pass	Pass
3♡	Pass	Pass	Double
All Pass			

Three hearts doubled was the final contract, and Gilda joyfully led the ace of spades. Prissy tabled her dummy. Maura took one look at that dummy and the usual serenity drained from her face. "Priscilla," her stern remonstration silenced the table, "How in Heaven's name can you bid three hearts with only two pieces? Don't you know The Law of Total Tricks? Have you lost your ever-loving mind?"

Prissy shrank. She never had a good answer when Maura quoted from her bridge readings. Gilda glibly shifted to a trump, and when Eileen showed out, Maura blanched whiter than a three-day-old corpse. Struggling on, she played dummy's king of diamonds to Eileen's ace. Eileen (having finally ordered from the waitress) cashed the king and queen of spades, as Gilda threw low clubs. Eileen then played her last spade for Gilda to ruff. Leading another trump, Gilda was able to hold Maura to only her four trump tricks.

Maura was livid. In one fell swoop she had gone from defending two spades with eight combined trumps, to declaring three hearts with six combined trumps. Down five for minus 1100. Maura was very annoyed with her partner, with Gilda, with bridge, and with herself. Maura simply hated to lose.

* * * * * * * * * *

After another very long day, Ford dragged his body home. He was fumbling unsuccessfully with the door lock when the phone began to ring. Evidently, he had forgotten to turn his answering machine on before he left, because the phone continued to ring with a car salesman's tenacity. He got the door open, left it hanging, and jogged across the room to the phone. "Hello," he answered, slightly off-balance.

"Are you still alive?" Meyer's voice resonated through the wire. "And do you still have a job?"

"Hang on a sec." Ford dropped the phone and went back to close the door. "Yeah, I'm still alive. And still employed, believe it or not." Ford was as surprised as anyone. "But I do have a theory as to why I am still employed," he said.

"Okay, I'm game. Why?" Meyer loved theories of all flavors.

"My theory is this: I am still employed because Vanessa likes to scream at me. I am not really a paid *bridge* professional, I am a professional *whipping boy*." Ford chuckled, too tired to be outraged.

"What, specifically, made you come to this realization today, Ford?" Meyer had realized it some time ago, and he was itching to know how it finally sunk in to Ford's thick but decent skull.

"I'm at the club; Vanessa and I are playing. Naturally, we are having a horrible game; what else is new. No matter. So we sit down against two of the regulars there, Prissy and Maura. Both very sweet, but one of them really drives me nuts. As fate operates in my small corner of the world, the one that drives me absolutely crazy with her voice, her bidding and her ludicrous questions, is the one that ends up screwing me over in a bridge hand. The best part is, that it's totally inadvertent. I think she missorted her hand, or some such." Ford was beginning to see the humor in the horror of this job with Vanessa.

"The hand, maestro," Meyer called out.

"Yes. Prissy opened one notrump (15-17), and I was holding:

♠ K 5 3
♡ J 10 8 3
◇ Q 10 2
♣ 8 5 2

"Naturally, I passed, and Maura raised to three notrump, ending the auction. I led the jack of hearts. Dummy came down and I saw:

171

```
         ♠ A J 10
         ♡ K 2
         ◇ A J 9 4
         ♣ 10 7 6 3
♠ K 5 3
♡ J 10 8 3
◇ Q 10 2        ☐
♣ 8 5 2
```

"Prissy looked across the table, sputtering, 'Oh, thank you partner. I, well, just wasn't quite sure . . .' As you might expect, Meyer, I cut that little exchange short."

"I hope you were nice, Ford," Meyer said maternally.

"I was very nice. I smiled and asked firmly if she was ready to play now. She was. She played the heart king from dummy. Vanessa, who, having ripped my head off about six times over the course of the last three boards, won the ace. Prissy, who has never falsecarded in her life, followed with the seven. My lovely partner, an executioner in the French Revolution, continued with the queen of hearts, on which Prissy dropped the nine. Now, genius that I am, I know that Prissy is out of hearts, and that she has all the remaining high cards. Right?"

"Well, right. You had six points, dummy had 13, and partner had just shown six, right?"

"Yep. That makes 25 points, so, using my great mathematical abilities, I deduced that Prissy must have the remaining 15 for her strong notrump. In fact, she was probably looking at something like:

♠ Q 9 8
♡ 9 7
◇ K 8 6 5
♣ A K Q J

"No troubles so far. I figured her for close to that hand. Having played against this woman a hundred times in the last two months, I know that as soon as she gets the lead, she'll easily take the rest of the tricks. She has the ol' finesse proclivity. Loves to take the finesse. She'll even try to make one up if there isn't one there. As a note, Meyer, we hear about her finesses unceasingly between hands," Ford grumbled.

"She's proud of her finesses. That's okay, Ford," Meyer reminded him gently.

"Meyer, I'm proud of my baseball team, too, but I don't talk about it between hands. It's very distracting. How would you like it if I relived every highlight of the last Marlins game *between hands*. Really, you have to draw the line. Discussing an issue with partner is one thing, but save your glory days for after the game. Plus, if you are the unlucky sod who happens to still be playing a round and sitting next to her, you get totally sidetracked." This was a pet peeve of Ford's.

"Speaking of sidetracked, press on." Meyer knew Ford would go on all day, given encouragement.

"So anyway, I knew she would take some finesses and scoop all the tricks in spades, diamonds, and clubs. But, after my heart lead, we were in the wonderful position of being able to take the first five heart tricks. My wicked partner could have made it somewhat easier on me by taking her ace of hearts at trick one, then leading back a *low* heart. I would capture declarer's nine with my ten, cash the eight, and then we would easily run the suit.

"No rest for the weary, Meyer. She cashed the ace and the queen without the trace of a thought. Fortunately, I knew Vanessa's heart suit was ace-queen-six-five-four. After she cashed her ace and queen I had to watch my step. If I had carelessly played my three, the hearts would block. I'd be left with the ten-eight which would block the suit and Vanessa's six-five-four would not all take tricks. After we'd cashed only four heart tricks, we would have to surrender. I carefully unblocked my eight. All we needed was Vanessa, the screaming mimi, to play one of her low ones to my ten. I'd lead the three back to her to set the old contract:

MAURA
♠ A J 10
♡ K 2
◊ A J 9 4
♣ 10 7 6 3

FORD
♠ K 5 3
♡ J 10 8 3
◊ Q 10 2
♣ 8 5 2

VANESSA
♠ 7 6 4 2
♡ A Q 6 5 4
◊ 7 3
♣ 9 4

PRISSY
♠ Q 9 8
♡ 9 7
◊ K 8 6 5
♣ A K Q J

174

"So all is well. Vanessa took her ace and queen of hearts, and on the second round, I unblocked my eight. She played the four of hearts and Prissy threw a spade. Maura, Prissy's partner, slowly looks up and says dejectedly, 'No hearts, partner?' At which point Prissy checks her hand for hearts. Good thing for her, too. She had a couple of hearts mixed in with the diamonds. Her actual hand was:

♠ Q 9 8
♡ 9 7 ⑥⑤
◇ K 8
♣ A K Q J

"Well, don't you know. One man's poison is another man's candy, whatever that saying is. After Prissy corrected her play, which she was legally entitled to do, the whole picture looked much different. We would be running the New York marathon before we were going to run those five heart tricks. No, we were headed straight for a big, round zero. Prissy moved the two little hearts out of the 'diamond slot' and plopped the heart five on Vanessa's four. I took my ten and meekly tried my last heart, the three, which lost to Prissy's six-spot. My day was turning out beautifully. Prissy took some finesses, came out with ten tricks and a top score. The real deal was:

MAURA
♠ A J 10
♡ K 2
◇ A J 9 4
♣ 10 7 6 3

FORD
♠ K 5 3
♡ J 10 8 3
◇ Q 10 2
♣ 8 5 2

VANESSA
♠ 7 6 4 2
♡ A Q 4
◇ 7 6 5 3
♣ 9 4

PRISSY
♠ Q 9 8
♡ 9 7 ⑥ ⑤
◇ K 8
♣ A K Q J

"At every other table, the auction was identical, one notrump-three notrump. Everyone in my seat led the heart jack. All the East's won the ace and the queen, and returned the four through declarer's nine-seven. Without exception, all Wests took the eight and ten to secure the first four tricks. So aside from our table, the board was flat at three notrump making only three." Ford paused to hear Meyer laughing hysterically on the other end of the line.

"Looks like you were taken by one of the best *Rueful Rabbit* plays in history," Meyer eked out between laughs.

"Funny to you. Vanessa, Satan's enchanting Bride, has zero humor. She started with that 'Why did we get the lowest score on this board?' which I assumed to be a rhetorical question. Then Vanessa wanted to know if 'Prissy was paying you, *Mr. Maddox?*' Then she ranted that she wished someone else was paying me, because she was tired of wasting money. It was all I could do to refrain from saying, 'Yeah, me too.' Basically, she went though all of her usual histrionics, then her head turned into a big green snake and I went home."

"Do you feel like you two are prepared for the Nationals?" Meyer asked.

"Well, we won that regional a couple of weeks ago, which qualified us to play in the Blue Ribbons. I don't think that translates to prepared, though, do you?" Ford replied.

"If she can control her temper, you are as prepared as you will ever be," Meyer remarked.

"Yes, and there's the rub. Her temper. I hate my job, Meyer. I can't do this much more," Ford sighed deeply.

"Listen, see how you feel about working with Vanessa after you get back from the Nationals," he advised.

"You mean see if I can drum up some new business," Ford corrected.

"Yep. Precisely. Talk to you later, I've got to go," Meyer said, and signed off.

* * * * * * * * *

"Rimmon, here," the voice gruffed into the phone.

"Hello, I'm looking for an R. Rimmon." Hereford was business-as-usual.

"And I'm looking for a winning lottery number," the voice answered.

Rankled, Hereford persisted, "I have a job for R. Rimmon."

"What kind of job?"

"You are a private investigator, are you not?" Hereford interrogated.

"On Mondays and every other Thursday." The cavalier voice flipped the words like pancakes.

Hereford's blood pumped through his veins as the curses pounded through his brain. "I find your attitude deplorable." His haughty voice attempted to assert control.

The voice on the phone would not be controlled. Having dealt with a million Hereford's in its life, it had no fear. This voice knew that information was far more powerful than either money or status; this voice knew the bottom line. "But you're still on the phone," Rimmon's gruff voice bullied. "That says to me you got an urgent problem." He paused just a second for that to sink in, then continued, "We both know there's only two guys in this city that can get this kind of job done right. Looks to me like you can't go to the other P.I. in town." He paused again. "Reason . . . maybe you know him and you don't want him to know your business. Maybe he knows your target, so you don't entirely trust him. Or maybe you just didn't get that far in the phone book, hmm?"

Hereford's mind stopped dead in its tracks. He chuckled softly to himself and lamented that this Rimmon character wasn't his bridge partner. "What does the 'R' stand for?" Hereford asked.

"Roc, as in Rocco," the gravelly voice replied.

"Okay, Roc," Hereford said pragmatically, "all of the above is true. It is urgent. The other P.I. does know the mark. And, I can make it worth your while."

"Uh-huh. Time is money," Rimmon stated blandly.

"Insight from a guy named Roc. Well, hell, I've seen worse days, I guess. But before we continue, do you know the other P.I. I'm talking about?" Hereford asked.

"Meyer? Course I know Meyer. Meyer an' me work together plenty. All the time. Professional courtesy an' all that."

"Is that going to compromise your working for me?"

"Chief, much as I love Meyer, you're paying my bills. Clear?" Rimmon said plainly.

"Clear to me as long as it's clear to you," Hereford confirmed.

"Crystal clear. What's the job?"

"First things first. Can you do this job immediately?" Hereford asked, feeling the pinch of anxiety.

"For the right price I can do it yesterday." Rimmon was blasé.

"Don't you worry about the price. Just listen carefully. . . ."

* * * * * * * * *

"What do we play over the opponents' one no-trump?" asked Prissy, competing with the hum of four great jet engines. It was just her luck that the in-flight movie equipment was inoperative. She had tried feigning sleep, but her attempt at simulating overpowering drowsiness at 11 in the morning was not very convincing. Her third and last hope was to restrict the conversation with Maura entirely to bridge. This plan turned out to be 50% effective—the 50% contributed by Prissy, herself. For, in response to Prissy's notrump question, Maura, deep in her unique fantasyland and staring into her club soda, gave voice to her own thoughts. "I'm certain the vents aren't working properly. We are almost surely breathing in the air everyone else is breathing out. Think of the germs, the pollutants, the poisons. If you just consider the bacteria in this soda glass . . ."

Prissy's mind raced as Maura's mouth rhapsodized. It was inexorably dawning on Miss Priscilla that even bringing home an event title would not make this trip worthwhile.

". . . why, my mucus membranes must be under tremendous stress in this cramped space . . ."

Prissy just couldn't take another two hours of The Tumor And Cyst Show. She had humored Maura for years, but she *was* reaching her limit. *Maybe we'll crash*, she thought to herself. *Now, there's a trade-off worth considering.*

Rigged Bridge

Clouds of stale, smokey air tumbled out into the hallway before Ford Maddox could close the heavy hotel door on his goodnights. He and Meyer had been trying to escape for an hour from Vanessa's suite. Her petite avian form vibrated with nervous energy, and her ceaseless chatter permeated the room. She was "sooo glad the national tournament was being held in Chicago this time," she said as she puffed on a skinny menthol cigarette, because she "absolutely loooved Chicago." She felt "so at home here," she insisted, and lit up another cigarette. Finally, Ford stood up from the sofa and announced, unequivocally, that he had to get some sleep. Ford and Meyer departed.

Halfway down the hall, Meyer turned to Ford and asked, "Does she smoke that much at the club?" A chain smoker would have suffocated in that room.

Ford sighed deeply. "No, she doesn't smoke at all while we're playing. I'm guessing that she's really nervous about playing tomorrow."

"Well, that's good, isn't it? She'll be a little humbled." Meyer thought this was a pretty good assessment of what usually happened to neophytes at the Nationals.

"Yes, you'd think so. But no, Vanessa is different. When she's nervous or feels uncomfortable, it just turns into anger. Do not pass Go, do not collect $200. Pure anger. I can't take much more of this, dealing with her," Ford declared.

"You're thinking of terminating this contract?" Meyer asked.

"Yeah," Ford's voice drifted. He felt in many respects it was a lack of professionalism. On the other hand, she was ruining his quality of life. And the purpose of money, after all, was to improve the quality of life. He'd rather play rubber bridge for a living. "I think after we get knocked out of this event, I'll tell her she's got to find another pro." He was not looking forward to that conversation.

"How do you think she'll take it?" Meyer was concerned.

"You know, the usual theatrics. The righteous indignation, the rage," Ford sighed. "What a waste of energy," he commented.

They rode the elevator down to their floor in silence. Stepping out, Meyer turned to the left, Ford to the right. "See ya in the morning," Meyer's drowsy voice faded as he walked away.

"Okay," Ford said. Ford walked lethargically down the dimly lit hallway, his eyes fixed in a meditative gaze on the blue and green flecks in the gray carpet. Why were these hallways always so poorly lit? Was this supposed to be mood lighting? What mood do you need to be in when you're walking down the hall? Frustrated with his current predicament, he slid the plastic key into its slip, went into the room, shed his clothes and crawled into bed. Nothing more to do tonight, he thought, as he passed into sleep.

Parson had been in Hereford's room since early afternoon. Hereford was checked in, but nowhere to be found. Parson, accustomed to waiting for Hereford, had ordered a very tasty room service dinner, complete with a half bottle of wine and chocolate mousse cake for dessert. He had reviewed the bridge system notes, read the paper and phoned his mother. Lying on the couch propped up by several pillows, he had just filled in number six-across in the *New York Times* crossword puzzle when Hereford burst in.

"I see you've made your pleasure my priority," Hereford patronized.

Parson looked at him like he had three heads. They went through this at every Nationals. Parson met Hereford at the tournament. One of Hereford's assistants checked them both in and Parson waited for Hereford in his suite. Hereford liked it that way; he said he didn't want to have to hunt for Parson. Parson suspected this little waiting game had more to do with power than any particular convenience, but he thought of it as just one more leg of the journey. Like being in an airport with better food and more comfortable seats.

"I have some good news for you, my dear boy. I have once again succeeded in saving you from yourself," Hereford gloated. *It's not myself I'm worried about*, Parson quipped to himself. Parson, having said absolutely nothing since Hereford walked in, only blinked.

"Aren't you going to ask how?" Hereford insisted. Parson assumed that was a rhetorical question and continued to say nothing. Hereford went on, disregarding his employee's apparent apathy. Having taken off his shoes, Hereford now paced feverishly around the suite, exuding fiendish energy. He went to the bar fridge and snatched a cold bottle of water.

"What? No ice?" he surveyed. "Did you use all the ice?" he barked. Again, Parson knew, not a question that really required answering. Hereford would eventually find the ice, in the ice bucket, on the bar table. Hereford poured the water into a glass, tossed in a couple of cubes, and began the furious swirling and clacking routine, which Parson always likened to Captain Queeg and his steel balls. Hereford stopped, mid-stride, and looked directly at Parson. "In light of your brilliant failure to gain access to the League's computer so we could input our own hands," he began icily, "I've arranged the next best thing. Of course you know that the computer-generated bridge hands are printed up on paper for each session," Hereford began.

"The hand records. Sure, that way we can go over all of your mistakes after the session," Parson played along.

"Parson," Hereford smiled gleefully, "I guess you've forgotten. I don't make mistakes. I'm the boss. But in any case, we will be getting copies of the hand records *before* the game. Giving you, Parson, ample opportunity to study them." Triumph radiated from Hereford's pores.

"Hereford, how did you manage that?" Parson was impressed.

"Let's just say I did. I told you it could be done, if you put your mind to it. You know the reason you're fat? You lie around too much." Hereford had waited all day to offer that bit of insight, and he felt much better

184

having said it. He continued, excited, "Okay, when we get the hand records, I'll make sure you have a copy. We will discuss them in person exclusively. We cannot discuss them on the phone, just in case . . . " He began listing all the possibilities and contingencies of this aspect of the scheme, exploring all the ramifications and concocting spy scenarios, flavored with paranoia.

Cops and robbers, Parson chuckled to himself. The C.I.A. and the undercover operation, "Hands On." Hereford, usually a well-grounded, hard-ass manipulator, occasionally left the real world for the world of his fantasy. During these fits, as Parson liked to call them, it was best to quietly play along. Every once in a while, Parson had a sharp desire to inject a needle of reality into the swollen balloon of Hereford's megalomaniacal fantasies, but fortunately the desire passed quickly. Parson would be fired immediately for such a betrayal. He tuned back in to hear Hereford relaying his instructions.

". . . Since you are the pro, you will memorize the hands and give me instructions," Hereford snapped imperiously. "I will familiarize myself with the hands, but not in too much depth. You will do the labor and I will manage the logistics," Hereford concluded.

"Okay, Hereford," Parson appeased. "How will I get the hands?"

"Don't concern yourself with that. You'll get them. Now get out of my room, I need to rest. Unlike you, I worked today." His demeaning voice filled the air.

Right, this is my idea of a vacation, Parson thought, like getting life in Alcatraz. Parson picked up his *Times* and headed to his own room. He finished the crossword in a hot bath, a feat it had taken him many years to master. The key was to avoid getting your hands wet while stepping into the tub. Once your hands were wet, even if you tried to dry them, it was impossible to get through the puzzle without drips puckering the paper and smearing the pencil. Parson had discovered that there were only two ways to avoid wet hands. Running the bath while sitting in the tub sacrificed the initial sensation of the hot bath engulfing your body. The alternative was to step into the full bath, lowering yourself into the water slowly with your forearms. Great concentration was necessary because the natural impulse was to plunge your hands into the water and pull the water over yourself. On many occasions, Parson had succumbed to that temptation: on those occasions he completed soggy crosswords.

Content, Parson padded off to bed. Still no bridge hand records, he noticed, and went to sleep.

Morning arrived, as bridge tournament mornings do, replete with optimistic enthusiasm and fear of complete failure. Each player knows this is the beginning of a long grind of difficult competition; each player believes in the possibility of triumph; each player has his own way of handling the stress. Ford went jogging early this morning, lamenting the approaching day. Meanwhile, Parson was ordering pancakes, two scrambled, side of sausage well-done, and coffee with cream, please. Hereford had dialed his office and was joyfully belittling one of his employees at a high decibel. Standing in a damp towel in front of the mirror, Vanessa applied her makeup and harangued the hotel maid mercilessly to press her blouse. The maid would not abandon her housekeeping duties, and Vanessa tried bullying. It was all for naught. The maid, born and raised in Wichita, Kansas, finally enlisted her college Spanish classes to create the subterfuge of 'No comprendo.' As Vanessa began to rail about immigration policy for the last thirty years, the maid slipped out.

The less-experienced players all went through similar routines and crises. Their expectations might be lower (and yet, less realistic), but the butterflies were the same. And so, Prissy and Maura, in adjoining rooms, sipped tea and prepared for their first Nationals as partners. Although they could play in most of the events, they had never won a Regional, and so, were not eligible to compete in the Blue Ribbon Pairs. They *could* watch this event however, and what fun it was going to be kibitzing the international luminaries of the bridge world competing in the premier pairs title. What stories they would be able to bring back to the girls.

At 12:30 p.m. the players started to congregate noisily at the playing site. They had to buy entries, fill out convention cards, get coffee and soda, and socialize. Vanessa appeared somewhat disoriented when Ford found her. He got her some coffee, walked her through the entry-buying, and then showed her how to find her seat. This is the least I can do, he thought, hearing the softest whisper of guilt in his ear.

Parson went downstairs, got the entry, filled out two convention cards—one for himself and one for Hereford—and quickly found his way to the concession stand. Knowing it might be a while before he would be able to visit the stand again, he purchased several snacks, a soda and a cup of coffee. Ten minutes before game time, Hereford surprised Parson, who was hovering over their starting table, deeply engrossed in a gigantic fudge-chocolate-chip cookie.

"Mercy, didn't you have breakfast?" Disgust filled Hereford's voice.

"It's lunchtime," Parson said sourly.

"Hmm. I trust you received the hand records. Is there anything we need to go over?" Hereford asked.

"Oh, one or two things. Let's walk outside. We have time," Parson replied and picked up the mutilated remains of his cookie.

"Must you bring that?" A sneer condemned Parson and the cookie.

"Yes," Parson snooted and scuttled off toward the door. Hereford stood motionless a moment, amazed by Parson's agility and speed. Quick reflexes like a bug, he mused, and followed. Returning from their clandestine conversation, they settled in and played several flawless rounds. Hereford and Parson were playing swimmingly, like champs. To Parson's delight, his skill was more than adequate, and they seldom used their illicit knowledge. Parson felt the urge to point this out to Hereford. A bridge professional for many years, Parson knew that the key to bridge success was unflappable concentration on each hand. He had tried explaining this to Hereford, but Hereford obstinately refused to listen. Hereford insisted that it was the brilliant plays that won the match. No, Parson argued, it was the brilliant plays that got written up in the paper. Consistent plays won the match.

Deal after deal confirmed this, Parson thought to himself and casually picked up the next hand:

Vul: E-W   HEREFORD
Dlr: West   ♠ Q 5 2
                 ♡ A Q 10
                 ◇ Q 10 7 5
                 ♣ 9 6 4

                 PARSON
                 ♠ A J 10 9 8 6
                 ♡ J 4 3
                 ◇ K 8 3 2
                 ♣ —

WEST	NORTH	EAST	SOUTH
	HEREFORD		PARSON
1♣	Pass	1NT	2♠
3♣	3♠	4♣	4♠
All Pass			

Aware that he might have to account for his bidding before this event was over, Parson dashed off an impromptu explanation in his mind. Four spades made perfect sense in light of Parson's club void, coupled with the opponent's big club fit. After all, Parson could explain, I inferred Hereford's cards were outside of clubs.

West began by leading the heart seven. Parson inserted the heart ten from dummy, losing to East's king. East then tried the club king, foiled by Parson's ruff.

Parson was grateful for East's play of the club king, as it eased the justification for his next move. Even though Parson had the blueprint of the deal memorized, he still enjoyed the art of argument—justifying the unusual but plausible line of play. This was what separated the wheat from the chaff. Knowing from the bidding that the hearts had to be 4-3, Parson crossed to dummy in hearts and led the queen of spades. East played low, and Parson went up with the ace!

East, Parson reasoned, had already shown up with the heart king, and undoubtedly, the club queen lurked alongside the club king. The spade king too? No, not with that one-notrump response. Too many points.

Parson satisfyingly watched the singleton spade king tumble down, and turned his attention to diamonds. Using his previous high-card point reasoning, he deduced that West must have the diamond ace. He also knew the lay of the hearts. East would have responded one heart (not one notrump) with a four-card heart suit, and West would have bid hearts if he had five. So, East must have three hearts, leaving West with four. West's bidding showed six cards in clubs, so West had to be 1-4-2-6 with a doubleton ace of diamonds. After drawing the other trumps, Parson led a swaggering diamond to dummy's queen, which held. A diamond came darting back, nine from East, low from Parson, and the ace fell for a very gratifying plus 450. Another hand won with naked skill. What a waste it was to have hand records when one was as talented as Parson.

Vul: E-W   HEREFORD
Dlr: West   ♠ Q 5 2
                  ♡ A Q 10
                  ◊ Q 10 7 5
                  ♣ 9 6 4

WEST   EAST
♠ K   ♠ 7 4 3
♡ 9 8 7 2   ♡ K 6 5
◊ A 4   ◊ J 9 6
♣ A J 8 7 5 3   ♣ K Q 10 2

                  PARSON
                  ♠ A J 10 9 8 6
                  ♡ J 4 3
                  ◊ K 8 3 2
                  ♣ —

WEST	NORTH	EAST	SOUTH
	HEREFORD		PARSON
1♣	Pass	1NT	2♠
3♣	3♠	4♣	4♠
All Pass			

Ford and Vanessa had not been playing swimmingly. Flounderingly was more like it. Leaning
towards drowning, really. While Parson was joyously
racking up an overtrick in four spades, Vanessa, East on
the same board, but at a different table, had mortgaged
her intuition. She had doubled *her* opponents in *three*
spades; though they made only three, Vanessa had to
scrape her score off the bottom of the barrel.

The Contessa was very nervous. And like her
happiness, sadness, pensiveness and relief, her nervous-
ness manifested itself as anger. Her indiscreet public

snipes had been tearing at Ford all day. She hadn't realized the breadth of his renown. Bridge players had been talking and joking with Ford all afternoon, without a remote curiosity for who she was. This annoyed her thoroughly. She promptly adjusted, however; she made it a point to inform every one of these people that Ford worked for her. Over the years, Ford had developed a reasonable tolerance for people's peculiarities—except for this one. The putrid flavor of this particular power trip gagged Ford. It was far too reminiscent of his father to be overlooked. Last night's discomfort about ending this partnership had dissipated into healthy resolve. Enough. This would be the last event they played together. The worse things seemed, the worse they got. Ford and Vanessa moved to the next table and apparently the North-South pair was still out in the hallway having a discussion. Then Ford glanced up to see Hereford and Parson walking towards the table. Ford almost laughed out loud at the perversity of it all. Unbelievable.

The jousting began the instant Hereford's rear was in the chair. "A rematch with my favorite little lady who believes she plays better than I do. We can make a side wager, if you would like. I'll bet you my hotel bill. I'm in the Presidential Suite, love," Hereford baited.

"Of course you are, dear," Vanessa volleyed with her most condescending voice. "I'm in the Ambassador's Suite, and I'm told it has the best view in the hotel."

"I don't care if you can see all the way to friggin' *Canada*, how about a wager?"

Vanessa said nothing and pulled her cards out of the board.

"I thought not," Hereford smirked.

"Let's play," Ford said grumpily.

"Just seeing if your client had any faith in you, son," taunted Hereford.

"Faith, prayer, and God's will won't help us against you, Hereford. Not unless we *all* play with marked cards," Ford said wearily, as he sorted his hand.

Vul: N-S
Dlr: South

HEREFORD
♠ 6
♡ Q J 9 8
◇ A 8 3 2
♣ J 7 6 5

FORD
♠ K J 10 9 2
♡ 6
◇ J 5
♣ A 9 4 3 2

VANESSA
♠ 8 7 4 3
♡ 5 3
◇ K Q 10 7
♣ K 10 8

PARSON
♠ A Q 5
♡ A K 10 7 4 2
◇ 9 6 4
♣ Q

WEST	NORTH	EAST	SOUTH
FORD	HEREFORD	VANESSA	PARSON
—	—	—	1♡
2♡*	4♡	4♠	5♡
Pass	Pass	Double	All Pass

* = Spades and a minor

Parson opened one heart, and Ford bid two hearts. This was Michaels, one of the few conventions

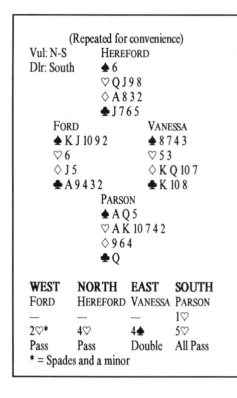

(Repeated for convenience)

Vul: N-S   HEREFORD
Dlr: South ♠ 6
            ♡ Q J 9 8
            ◇ A 8 3 2
            ♣ J 7 6 5

FORD   VANESSA
♠ K J 10 9 2   ♠ 8 7 4 3
♡ 6   ♡ 5 3
◇ J 5   ◇ K Q 10 7
♣ A 9 4 3 2   ♣ K 10 8

            PARSON
            ♠ A Q 5
            ♡ A K 10 7 4 2
            ◇ 9 6 4
            ♣ Q

WEST	NORTH	EAST	SOUTH
FORD	HEREFORD	VANESSA	PARSON
—	—	—	1♡
2♡*	4♡	4♠	5♡
Pass	Pass	Double	All Pass

* = Spades and a minor

Vanessa had actually deigned to discuss with him, showing spades and a minor. Hereford jumped eagerly to the heart game, and Vanessa bid four spades. Parson pressed on with a pushy five-heart bid. This was passed around to Vanessa, who, seemingly oblivious, doubled. *She's playing by "feel" again*, Ford thought.

Actually, five hearts might have been a sacrifice. Parson knew the hands, and he knew that four spades might make. Sure, he could have easily led a club against four spades. After winning the spade ace, he could simply cross to his partner in a red suit. Then he'd have to rely on Hereford to give him a club ruff to defeat the contract—but why rely on Hereford? Instead, he placed his confidence in Vanessa misdefending five hearts. He assumed he'd get a spade, not a diamond lead. Sure enough, Ford led the spade jack. Parson still appeared to have two diamonds and a club to lose, but he knew that Vanessa would help him out.

194

He won the spade lead in hand and crossed to dummy in hearts to play a low club. Vanessa, who knew her maxims well, played second hand low. Ford captured the club queen with the ace and shifted, but too late, to diamonds. Parson won the diamond ace, ruffed a club, crossed in trumps, and ruffed another club, felling Vanessa's king. The jack of clubs was now established for a diamond pitch, five hearts doubled bid and made.

Vanessa's face spasmed, her eyes narrowing into ovals of red rage. Taking aim, she fired her venom across the table at Ford, "You haven't made the right lead all day. Why lead a spade from the king-jack? Couldn't you work out that I had diamonds?"

"I'm sorry, Vanessa," Ford's sarcasm pared the meat from the bone, "my Ouija board broke last week, and I didn't get it back from the repair shop yet. In any case, I'm not sure exactly why the absence of a diamond lead paralyzed your powers of deductive reasoning. After all, if my minor was diamonds, we weren't beating this hand. I guess it would be reasonable for you to figure that I had clubs. It is possible, from your seat," he said with controlled contempt, "to see what might happen if you played low on the club. I agree, it's hard to see when you're busy mentally crucifying your partner, but if you played the club king, Parson couldn't set up a club trick and he would have to lose two diamonds. Even if you got your wish of an opening diamond lead, declarer would duck the first round of diamonds and you'd still have to rise with the club king at the appropriate moment. It is possible to envision the need to rise with king. Possible," he concluded witheringly, "but not necessarily probable."

195

Vanessa clenched her talons into fists, "You know you're fired!" she screeched.

"You know I quit," Ford irreverently grinned.

Glory Bids

Ford had just returned from an invigorating morning run. He saw the sunlight saunter through the window, slip embarrassingly off the window ledge and land on the chair just below it. His body was filled with contentment; he was at peace with the world. It was the third and final day of the Blue Ribbon Pairs. Ford had felt as if he had shed a heavy weight when he and Vanessa got knocked out on the first day. He showered and called Meyer to meet him downstairs at the hotel cafe for the buffet breakfast. His mind listed the tasty possibilities: fluffy pancakes, scrambled eggs, crispy bacon, eggs benedict smothered in Hollandaise, and lots of fresh juice and fruit.

The white wicker furniture of the hotel cafe seemed trapped by the overgrown, mauve, floral wallpaper. As Ford walked in, he noticed the pinkness of everything, but seeing the buffet table piled high with food put all concerns of pink in their proper perspective. He followed the host to the table, flung his newspaper down, grabbed a plate, and began heaping the food onto his dish. Meyer strolled up behind Ford and caught him eating chunks of fruit as he went.

"Hungry, Maddox?"

"Had a great run," he said, swallowing. "I'm ravenous."

"I think you're just thankful to be relieved from your tour of duty with the Contessa," Meyer analyzed, and picked up a plate.

Ford went back to his seat, and with something akin to reckless abandon, he devoured his breakfast.

Meyer joined him, though with decidedly less zeal. Hunger temporarily sated, Ford leaned back in his chair. He would have belched had he been in a Jersey diner. "Gathering your strength before the second attack?" Meyer grinned.

"Naturally. I have to be thoroughly prepared. I'm kibitzing Hereford and Parson again today, and I must be prepared for a long siege. Can't leave the table for a snack midway through. I might miss something," Ford halfway mocked himself.

"Again? You're going to watch them play bridge, all day, again? Why? There was nothing yesterday, you said." Meyer protested against what he considered a prodigious waste of time.

"I know what I said yesterday, but I am completely convinced they are cheating. They are cheating. I intend to find out how. For my own satisfaction." Ford wanted to close the subject.

Meyer bulldogged him. "They are cheating, but you still have no idea how. Moreover, you've seen nothing that even indicates that they are."

"Nothing? You call those unbelievably high scores nothing?" Ford pinched the words indignantly.

"Ahem, yes. Scores. Well, it's your day to waste, I guess. Penny and I will be enjoying ourselves, playing in a side game with the masses of other bridge players who are here to enjoy themselves. But, since I don't think you should be allowed to torture yourself all day looking for cheating in a room full of honesty, please join us for dinner. Breaks up the monotony of hunting for a needle in a haystack. Or, hunting for a needle that doesn't exist," Meyer ribbed.

"Laugh away, foolish, skeptical Meyer. I'm telling you, as sure as I sit here," Ford smiled confidently, "they are cheating."

"Because they have high scores?" Meyer objected.

"Haven't you heard the expression, 'Every dog has his day?'"

"They've had two days. Dogs don't have two days in this kind of event. The best these dogs can have is fleas. Period," Ford said resolutely. "I'm going early to get my kibitzer's seat," Ford said. He signed the check to his room and trekked off to the area where the Blue Ribbon Pairs was being held.

"Okay, have fun," Meyer called after him. "Just don't bring the fleas to dinner." Meyer beckoned the waitress for another cup of coffee and picked up the morning paper Ford had left on the table.

* * * * * * * * * *

Parson hated hotels. You could never get a good night's sleep. Inevitably, there were kids clamoring down the hallway, bawling and shrieking like freed demons. The people in the next room were going ten rounds because of something somebody's in-laws said to someone else, usually not even related. Or, they were making up after that fight, inflicting their noisy copulations on everyone within a five-mile radius, except, of course, the kids, who were screaming so loudly they couldn't hear an atom bomb. For Parson, the worst possible scenario was the most frequent: TV watchers. A practical man, Parson knew that neither fighting nor sex could go on forever, because someone would end up dead. The TV was another story altogether. Parson did not dislike all TVs. TVs in bars, peoples' homes, airports, all seemed fairly innocuous (save the programming). Hotel TVs and the People Who Watched Them. They were the pernicious kind. Hotel TVs were always permanently affixed to the wall directly behind the headboard of Parson's bed. This was a universal hotel room design, leading Parson to speculate that the competition for hotel room designers was minimal. The hotel TV itself suffered from its own design flaws. It had only two volumes, blaring and off, and it came with a broken remote control. Blaring would be okay, for 18 of the 24 hours, but the broken remote was enough to prompt a murder-suicide. What it meant was, tired after countless hours of TV watching, the TV watchers would simply fall asleep with the damn thing on, because they didn't want to get up and turn it off. Four o'clock in the morning would find Parson listening to the Home Shopping Channel in Spanish, cursing in English.

The beautiful thing was that on the best of nights, after you finally got to sleep, about 20 minutes after a Valium, you could get maybe four hours of sleep. The same room designer that bought the broken, two-volume TVs, chintzed on the curtains as well. Hotel windowware could no more keep out daylight than New York sewers could keep out rats. Three days in a hotel left Parson grouchy; at a ten-day tournament, he was homicidal.

It was ten o'clock in the morning and the finals of the Blue Ribbon Pairs would start in three hours. Sporting dark burgundy boxers and skin, Parson sat sipping coffee, light and sweet, eating danish. After his fifth goo-filled pastry, he turned his mind to the business at hand. He and Hereford were in second place from yesterday. He smiled to himself. Hereford's plan was working splendidly. Since the event began, Parson had received a copy of the daily hand records with his morning coffee. Having no idea how Hereford had managed this, Parson was duly impressed. Hereford evidently didn't want to be seen anywhere in the vicinity under some lame pretense of "keeping his hands clean." Every day, the hand records showed up without a trace. Parson wondered whether, given the choice, Hereford would rather win by cheating or by honest methods. Cheating, Parson concluded, if it were accompanied by a really exciting scheme that screwed somebody in the process. No explaining people at all, he decided, and set himself to memorizing the hands.

As he worked, his mind wandered, and Mother, uninvited as usual, entered his thoughts. Mother questioned Parson as to how he could remember so many bridge hands, some of them from a decade ago. After all, he couldn't even remember the date of her gall bladder operation, she would remind him. This was always followed by the comment, 'A curious phenomenon, Peanut,' spoken in a voice that steamed the guilt out of otherwise crisp words. He would pleadingly answer that he had played literally thousands of bridge hands and that she had had only one gall bladder operation. On the days she was looking for a fight (which was the only time she ever brought this up), she would counter with the remark that the unique thing should stand out in the mind, not the commonplace. Usually, Parson would busy himself right about then to avoid telling her the obvious truth. Repeating the obvious truth to unwilling listeners was generally a bad idea.

His work done, Parson ambled downstairs for the one o'clock game start. Hereford strode over, forced a public smile upon his furrowed brow, and dropped his voice. "Everything set?"

"Yep. The first hand, bid Stayman," Parson said quietly and turned to walk to their table.

"Is that it?" Hereford queried.

"Nooo. One board at a time, like yesterday. Relax, okay?" Parson answered. They sat down at the table. Hereford took a deep breath and pulled his concentration down over his face like a steel helmet. Settled, he picked up the North cards.

HEREFORD
♠ Q 8 5 2
♡ A Q 10
♢ K 5 2
♣ 8 6 5

PARSON
♠ A 10 6 4
♡ K J 8
♢ A Q 10 6
♣ Q J

WEST	NORTH	EAST	SOUTH
	HEREFORD		PARSON
—	—	—	1NT
Pass	2♣	Pass	2♠
Pass	4♠	All Pass	

202

West led the ace, king, and a third round of clubs. Parson ruffed, and fired back a low spade towards dummy. West ducked smoothly, Parson played the queen, and East dropped the jack like a brick from a tower. Parson quietly folded up his cards and collapsed his eyelids heavily. His breathing slowed to an even pace. Everyone at the table shifted uncomfortably; it looked as though Parson had settled into a nice, long think. Hereford was the most uncomfortable of all, knowing Parson had nothing to think about. A thinking Parson was trouble in Paradise. In the second minute, Parson's left-hand opponent cleared his throat loudly, and with meaning. The third minute came and the solid mass of Parson hadn't twitched a nerve. By every estimation, he looked to be asleep. Finally, his left-hand opponent (afraid to wake a sleeping man, because he had been punched once) slammed the palm of his hand onto the table top. Parson lifted his eyelids and calmly said, "So sorry," and played another trump to his ace. When everyone else followed, he spread his hand.

Vul: None   HEREFORD
Dlr: South   ♠ Q 8 5 2
             ♡ A Q 10
             ◊ K 5 2
             ♣ 8 6 5

West	East
♠ K 7 3	♠ J 9
♡ 7 6 2	♡ 9 5 4 3
◊ J 9 8 3	◊ 7 4
♣ A K 4	♣ 10 9 7 3 2

             PARSON
             ♠ A 10 6 4
             ♡ K J 8
             ◊ A Q 10 6
             ♣ Q J

"You get the high trump, and I make the remaining tricks," Parson said plainly. East, who had made the excellent falsecard with the spade jack at trick four puckered his face sourly. East was annoyed that Parson made his game and scored 420, especially considering that most of the field would probably bid one notrump-three notrump leaving declarer fettered to eight tricks at best.

Buried by time pressure, the foursome quickly shoveled the cards back into the first board and dug the cards from the second. They plowed through the second hand without event, and East-West sprang up to switch for the next round. Parched, Ford left his kibitzer's seat and went in search of water. Hereford hulked his whole body menacingly over the flimsy bridge table and scowled, "What in the hell happened to you on the first hand? I thought you might have had a stroke and were temporarily paralyzed. We're lucky they didn't call the director for that kind of pointless delay. Well?"

"I was thinking of the possibilities of the hand, that's all," Parson mused.

"There *were* no possibilities," Hereford asserted.
"If you must know, there were. I was looking at:

HEREFORD
♠ Q 8 5 2
♡ A Q 10
◇ K 5 2
♣ 8 6 5

PARSON
♠ A 10 6 4
♡ K J 8
◇ A Q 10 6
♣ Q J

"After the ace, king and another club, I led a trump to the queen, and my right-hand opponent dropped the jack. I couldn't help thinking that the jack might be an honest card. My mind postulated that this might be the full deal:

HEREFORD
♠ Q 8 5 2
♡ A Q 10
◇ K 5 2
♣ 8 6 5

West
♠ K 9 7 3
♡ 7 6 2
◇ J 8 3
♣ A K 4

East
♠ J
♡ 9 5 4 3
◇ 9 7 4
♣ 10 9 7 3 2

PARSON
♠ A 10 6 4
♡ K J 8
◇ A Q 10 6
♣ Q J

(Parson's hypothetical deal)
(Repeated for convenience)

HEREFORD
♠ Q 8 5 2
♡ A Q 10
◇ K 5 2
♣ 8 6 5

West	East
♠ K 9 7 3	♠ J
♡ 7 6 2	♡ 9 5 4 3
◇ J 8 3	◇ 9 7 4
♣ A K 4	♣ 10 9 7 3 2

PARSON
♠ A 10 6 4
♡ K J 8
◇ A Q 10 6
♣ Q J

"Yes, Parson. And so what? What's to ponder over that?" Hereford failed to see any point whatsoever.

"The point is an artistic one that can only be appreciated by a highly refined aesthetic sensibility," Parson sneered. Who was Hereford to interfere with his heroic fantasies? "Considering the position after three rounds of clubs, and a spade to dummy's queen and East's jack, it would appear as though West had two 'certain' trump tricks left," Parson sniffed.

"You mean because he was left with king-nine-third behind declarer's ace-ten?" Hereford confirmed.

"Precisely. But, if West had the right shape, namely 4-3-3-3, the hand could still be made. Declarer—of course that's me—would simply cash three hearts and three diamonds, ending up in hand. West has to follow helplessly. One of the sexiest elimination plays I have seen recently, I might add." Parson cast a knowing smile across the table to Hereford. Baffled, Hereford stared blankly. Parson continued, "I exit with my last diamond in this three-card ending:

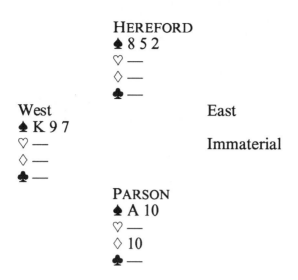

HEREFORD
♠ 8 5 2
♡ —
♢ —
♣ —

West
♠ K 9 7
♡ —
♢ —
♣ —

East

Immaterial

PARSON
♠ A 10
♡ —
♢ 10
♣ —

"Ha!" Parson expectorated, "West can take only one trump trick. Ten tricks made for declarer. Absolutely beautiful. A joyous hand!" Parson basked in the light of his own brilliance.

"You mean to tell me that's what you were thinking about during the hand?" Hereford was incredulous.

"Yes, indeed. A triumphant coup." Parson stretched his neck up proudly.

"You need help. That hand didn't exist." Hereford had the deep desire to slap some sense into Parson, but it would have caused a ruckus.

"Ah, but it could have. Fortunately we had the hand records, so we knew it didn't exist," Parson said.

"No, fortunately you play cards for a living and nobody's life depends on your discretionary abilities. Sick, sick, sick." Hereford knew Parson liked to grandstand, but he never knew it was this deep. Hereford decided that Parson was just a little crazier than he really needed to know about.

The Honorable Feast

"I think we're dressed all right," Penny said, peering from the bar into the restaurant.

"Well, I heard that this was the best Thai food in Chicago, but I didn't hear anything about a dress code." Ford followed her eyes. They seemed to be dressed okay to him.

Penny shrugged her shoulders. "Hey, the worst they can do is not let us in, right?" she said, and finished her glass of wine. Ford ordered another round.

The host motioned to them. They grabbed their drinks and found the table.

"Where's Meyer?" Ford had not seen him for some time now, and was wondering if he got lost between the door and the table. You never could tell with those private detectives.

"He went to make a phone call. He said to go ahead and order," Penny relayed.

Ford ordered more wine and a spicy crispy duck appetizer. Concerned that that might not be enough food to get him through to dinner, he added a large bowl of lemongrass and shrimp curry soup. The wine arrived, followed shortly by the food, and Ford wasted no time on amenities. "Meyer's not back. I'm eating. You should do the same; sometimes he's gone forever." But Penny was enjoying her wine, and after her third glass, had very little need for anything else.

Meyer made his way back to the table. "Hungry, Maddox?" he laughed and sat down.

"I've been working hard," Ford rejoined.

"Um-hm," Meyer surveyed, "very hard by the looks of your plate."

"You didn't happen to see the scores at halftime, did you?" Ford pushed.

"I did, in fact," Meyer said humbly.

"Don't you think it's just a tad odd that Hereford, man of impeccable integrity, and Parson, whose scruples are beyond reproach, have once again scored 60%? Even though yesterday they had 65% and 60%, and the first day they averaged over 60%? Wait—wait, Meyer, let me guess. Canines and calendars," Ford challenged.

"Huh?" Penny was lost.

"Meyer's theory is that Parson and Hereford are winning, due to a lucky streak, because 'Every dog has his day,'" Ford scoffed.

"For the first time this tournament, I have to say I think you're right. I think they are cheating," Meyer smiled graciously.

"Oh stop. I know you think this is ridiculous. No need to humor me, skeptical Meyer," Ford played.

"No, no. I thought you were a little paranoid at first, I confess. But, you were so dead set on this, I did some checking. Made a few calls ... ," Meyer admitted. Hey, if Ford was right, he was right.

"You called your buddy Roc?" Ford asked eagerly.

"Who's Roc?" Penny asked.

"He's a P.I. friend of mine," Meyer explained. "I did call him. He had some interesting information. Penny, I think you'll find this intriguing." Meyer's straight face suggested nothing.

Penny looked queasy.

"It seems," Meyer began, "that our good pal Parson is more of a computer whiz than he ever let on."

"Bill Gates look out," Ford quipped. "So, go on," he prompted.

"Evidently, he is the one who accessed the League computer and input the thirteen-hearts hand that made all the papers," Meyer revealed.

"What!" Penny sat bolt upright. "What do you mean he's the one who input that damn hand? That hand got me fired. That hand got me Vanessa, and fired again," she was outraged. "He knew about the deal generator, that s.o.b.," she said more to herself than anybody else.

"Deal generator? What are you talking about?" Meyer pressed.

"Oh. I went to his apartment, remember. He asked a lot of questions about the League's generator and the code. What a dirt-bag!" She was disgusted.

"Wait a sec, how did Roc figure out that Parson input that hand?" Ford questioned in disbelief. Meyer had pulled some good stunts in the past, but this took the cake.

"I had him check the hard drive on Parson's computer," Meyer boldly answered.

"He had a key to Parson's apartment? Or, you lent him your copy?" Ford grinned.

"Something like that." His ambiguity confirmed Ford's suspicions.

"So it is possible, that somehow, they have this event rigged so that they know the hands," Ford drove hard.

"It looks likely. But I doubt we'll be able to prove it." Meyer gave a slight shoulder shrug. "We're out of time; there's only one session left to go."

"Meyer, if we don't prove it today, it's going to continue. They'll just keep using whatever method they have to win," Ford pleaded urgently.

The color drained out of Penny's face and she took a large gulp of her pinot noir. Surprised, Meyer asked, "Penny, are you thirsty?"

"Uuh, I have something to say," she stammered.

"Let me guess, you like the wine?" Meyer teased. Having known her for many years, he knew she wasn't much of a drinker.

"I . . . uh . . . ," her voice tripped and disappeared down the hole of humiliation. "I h-h-helped them cheat," she finished. Tipping her head forward, she rested the bridge of her nose on the forefinger of her hand. Innocuous tears dripped silently onto the tablecloth. "I'm sorry," she whispered, "Hereford blackmailed me." Raising her eyes slightly, she feebly reached for the wine bottle.

"My father, the honorable Hereford Willis III, blackmailed you?" Ford confirmed. "He doesn't change. But tell me, what happened? How on earth did he blackmail you?" Ford was more curious than judgmental. He was endlessly amazed by his father's sphere of influence. That man could find out anything about anybody.

212

Penny was visibly relieved at Ford's kindness. "When I was in college," she coughed and snuffed her nose, "my boyfriend—actually, we talked about getting married—was a photographer. He loved to take pictures of me, nudes. Well . . . uh . . . some of them were pretty risque," she stammered, "you know, lewd."

"Yeah, well it would be hard for Hereford to blackmail you with travel pictures featuring you and the Eiffel Tower," Ford laughed.

Feeling that she had to explain herself, Penny continued, "I guess I should have known better because some of the poses were graphic, but . . . ," regret flooded her soft eyes, "he said it was very important to him. He said our intimacy would blossom," she could barely get the words out. "I really loved him. I thought we were going to get married."

"It's no big deal, Penny," Ford tried to calm her. Crying women made him nervous. "We've all done crazy stuff," he continued lightly, "if you think about it, on a scale of one to ten, it's not so bad. Not bad at all." If nothing else, Ford had succeeded in making himself feel better.

"So let me understand this," Meyer started grinding. "Hereford found these pictures? And contacted you how?"

"I don't know how he found the pictures. Who knows what riffraff he employs to dig up this kind of stuff? In any case, he sent a photo to me by e-mail, and threatened to post it all over the Internet, send it to my friends, and even my family." Penny was still horrified at the thought.

This information gathered, Meyer pressed for more. "So, how exactly did you help them cheat?"

"Hereford told me that he had to have the hand records in advance of the session. They usually print them up one session ahead of time. So I got him the hand records," Penny said.

"Nobody said anything?" Meyer puzzled.

Penny looked up and flashed a mischievous grin. "I still have a few old connections from my Memphis days."

"Okay, not to be callous here or anything, Penny," Ford wanted to move the discussion along. "We need to come up with a plan to stop them."

"There's no way to stop them now, they're on pace to win the event," Penny lamented.

"Ford, let's just alert the League and let them handle it," Meyer reasoned.

"No, Goddamit! I've heard too many of your lectures about my inherent apathy and laziness when it comes to participating in the bridge community. So I'm going to participate. I happen to know that the League is like any other bureaucracy. Left to themselves, they will drag their feet on this, worried about a lawsuit. The only way the League will act immediately is if they have to. As far as I'm concerned, we have to force their hand. We must make it impossible for them to ignore this, or to stall. I cannot personally stand to see my father cheat and win a title. No, I will stop Hereford and Parson— with you or without you. If even once people win by cheating, it ruins it for the rest of us," Ford reasoned passionately.

"Look, Ford, I know it pisses you off, but, you know, there have been other cheating scandals in bridge. Not many, but a couple, and bridge has survived," Meyer tried to calm the waters.

"Yeah. It survived, all right. Look at how it survived. People are very lax ethically because they rationalize to themselves: 'Well, it's not as if I'm cheating like Joe Blow did. I'm just encouraging my partner to the right contract.' Most of the time, people don't even *think* of it as cheating. That's because, in part, these organized cheating scandals make the continuum of cheating much too broad. They give people way too much room to rationalize their poor tempo, their eye contact, their head shakes, their voice inflections when they are trying to get their partner to do the right thing. 'I'm not *cheating*,' they tell themselves. 'It's not like a cough means spades and a sniff means clubs,'" Ford spoke fervently.

Meyer was quiet. "You're right, Maddox." One of Meyer's best attributes as a partner was his ability to admit being wrong. "Okay, let's think."

"Well, it's 9 p.m., so they've already played half the hands for tonight's session," Penny contributed.

"Oh yeah, this is being scored barometer style," Ford remembered. "So, all the hands are already sitting in the boards at every table. Everybody is playing the identical hands at the same time," Ford finished the thought out loud.

"It seems pretty clear to me. All we have to do is switch some deals," Meyer concluded.

"Well, we're going to have to talk to the head tournament director, and get him to help us," Ford said.

215

Penny swallowed hard. "I guess that means I'm going to have to tell my story again?"

"Unfortunately, I think that's the only way we can stop them. We can work something out with the directors; I don't think it will be a problem," Meyer comforted.

"So if we switch the deals, they will screw up the hands. Then we will know," Ford said.

"The League is going to want solid, hard proof, Ford. They're not going to accept anything less. I don't think that constitutes proof," Meyer warned.

"Okay . . . hmm," Ford fell into deep thought.

"What if they somehow admitted it?" Penny proposed.

"That would be proof. But why would they admit it in front of League members?"

"They might admit it to me," Penny intimated with a smile. "And I might have a tape recorder," she finished.

"That's it! That's what we have to do! But how will they admit it to you?" Ford was ecstatic with this possibility.

"I think at least one of them is going to be pretty upset that the deals got switched. That's as good as an admission," she asserted.

"You know, one other thing," Penny said as they were paying the check to leave, "I don't think the head director should switch the boards."

"Why not?" Meyer asked.

"I think I should do it. That way, they'll think I'm just helping with their scheme. And when they realize the boards are switched, they'll definitely know I did

216

it. Believe me, Hereford will have something to say to me about that," Penny spoke with certainty.

"Good point. Okay, that's the plan we'll go with. Let's get back to the tournament and find the director. You two are going to have to explain things; I've got to get in there and get my kibitzer's seat or Hereford and Parson will be suspicious," Ford rallied the troops.

"You think they'll notice?" Penny asked.

"I've been watching every move they've made for two days now. I've told them that I know they're cheating and that I'm going to prove it. It'll raise eyebrows if I don't come back at some point for the final session," Ford said.

* * * * * * * * *

"Well, that's it," Prissy called to Maura in the next room of their third-floor hotel suite, "I've moved our return flight reservations up. We have to be at O'Hare in two and a half hours." It hadn't been a terrible experience, but it had been disappointing for both ladies. After one week, they hadn't managed better than a section third in a morning side game, and even the kibitzing of the Blue Ribbon Pairs wasn't going well. All the big stars seemed to have the maximum allowable number of onlookers already seated around their tables. (How Prissy dreamed that she might one day, even for 15 minutes, be the central object of that adoring crowd.)

On their first off-day from bridge, Prissy had allowed herself to be dragged to Maura's colon specialist. It was in his office that both ladies received the news

217

which absolutely crushed Maura. Her health, apparently, was excellent, and the doctor considered her request for bypass surgery frivolous. It ate at Maura that not one of her doctors or friends could ever recognize or sympathize with her many aches and ailments.

To make the whole trip even more depressing, the entire tournament had been so ordinary and uneventful that they wouldn't even have any stories to tell the girls. They were both so unhappy that they had decided to leave Chicago ahead of time, without even attempting to watch the last session of the Blue Ribbons. They dreaded their first afternoon session back in Miami with nothing to tell Eileen, or Gilda, or the others. Well, at least they had made the trip. They would simply say they had attended the most predictable and unexciting Nationals ever.

The Trap

By the time the musketeers got things squared away with the officials, the evening session was almost over. Ford waited for a round change to take his kibitzer's seat behind Parson. Parson, entirely focused on the game, ignored Ford. Hereford looked over and said, "Glad you could make it for our big win tonight. I was afraid you were sulking and wouldn't show up."

"No, you're the main event here, and I wouldn't miss it for the world." Ford smiled and sat down.

"It's too bad you're not playing," Hereford baited.

"It's too bad you are," Ford parleyed.

"Hereford," Parson snapped, "be serious and focus. We have only two rounds to go." The round change complete, the entire room quieted their thoughts under a blanket of concentration. Ford settled back in his seat. He did not look up when Penny came into the room. With poise, she walked from table to table, switching the two boards for the final round. Parson, who was dummy this hand, stared hard at Penny. She looked back blankly and continued. His mind shivered suddenly with concern. He scanned Ford's face. Ford raised his eyes with questioning eyebrows, and Parson leaned over and whispered in his ear, "What's she doing?"

Ford replied, "I'm not sure. The other director got sick after dinner, and they tracked her down to take over." Parson nodded in acceptance, and Ford resumed his focus on the card play. To Ford, it seemed like the round took a lifetime.

At last, the call was made for the final round change. Hereford and Parson pushed their chairs back and got up. Hereford looked like he wanted to go to the concessions area, but Parson steered him instead to an unoccupied corner. As they whispered, Ford could see their stiff shoulders bending awkwardly under weight of the event.

"Remember Hereford, show two keycards on board 25 and lead a club on 26," Parson drummed his voice into Hereford's head.

"Yes, okay. Two keycards on 25, club on 26. By the way, why is Penny directing?" Hereford asked distractedly.

"Ford said the other director got sick." Parson's slit eyes narrowed further. "Does she have something to do with our plan?"

"*Our*? *My* plan. Yes, in fact she's an integral part of my plan," Hereford announced territorially.

"Does your plan call for her to suddenly be directing?" Parson pressed.

"No. But I'm sure that she's arranged this," Hereford spoke with Satan's confidence.

"Or she had a change of heart," Parson admonished.

"She wouldn't dare. With what I have on her, she would sell her soul first." Hereford's steel-blue eyes flashed with conquest.

Parson was not comforted. "Hereford, we are leading the event. Let's play these last two boards naturally; there is no doubt we will finish in the top two or three. That's amazing for a client pair. I don't know how you have orchestrated this plan so far, and I don't want to know, but I'm telling you, something strange is going on. Something smells in Denmark. Let's be safe. Fifty percent chance we win anyway," Parson urged.

"You are a spineless jellyfish. I designed this plan and it is foolproof. We stay with the plan, got it?" Hereford spat his words through clenched teeth.

"Okay, whatever," Parson conceded. "Two keycards now, and then lead a club on the last board." Hereford strode off, and worry spread across Parson's forehead. He remained standing where he was, thinking quickly. Even if this whole thing blows up, the League has nothing on us, he reasoned. As long as I can explain every move I make, and I can, they'll need hard evidence. They would need a signed confession. Knowing the likelihood of that, Parson relaxed a bit. Ford, watching this interplay, had not moved a muscle.

As Hereford and Parson took their East-West seats, Parson allowed himself a satisfied smile. He harbored a personal resentment against his final-round opponents. They had beaten him several times over the years, and adding insult to injury, one of them was a woman. She was considered the best woman player in the world; so mentally tough, she played like a man. Her partner was no slouch himself. He was a multi-time national champion, with a couple of world titles thrown in for flavor. It never ceased to amaze Parson that a woman could make it to the finals of these open events. He secretly believed they were cheating, because no player could be good enough to carry someone the entire event, and surely she was not pulling her weight. The knowledge that he was not only going to beat her, but to gloriously trounce her, sent adrenaline shooting through his veins. Aware that the last two deals were entirely in his control, he considered his opponents with an arrogance that rivaled Hereford's. His mind read the newspaper headlines all over the country; he'd give interviews to the bridge magazines explaining to the masses his keen bidding insight and superlative card play. Yes, these last hands, with his expert play, would undoubtedly be the most important, breathtaking ones of the tournament. *Shooting fish in a barrel*, he thought as he pulled his cards out of the board.

The simplicity of the first board glittered like glass in the summer sun:

HEREFORD	PARSON
♠ 6 4	♠ A K Q
♡ Q J 7 4 3	♡ A 10 9 8 5 2
◊ 4 2	◊ A K
♣ A K 8 7	♣ 9 2

Parson did not have to jump the same hurdles as the other players in this race. *They* had to concern themselves with the location of the king of hearts. If it was in the wrong place, you had to stop in a small slam. If there were no heart loser, you could bid and make seven. Knowing the hearts were 2-0 onside, Parson's hurdle was how to come up with an explanation for going slightly, but coincidentally, against the odds. He'd have to explain why he took the winning heart finesse and how he got to the seven level missing the king of trumps. With concern sitting on the stoop in the back of his mind, Par-

222

son had guided the bidding into a sequence that was beyond reproach, and quickly devised an explanation for anyone who might question him:

HEREFORD	PARSON
—	2NT
3◊*	3♡
4♣	4NT
5♡**	7NT
Pass	

* = transfer
** = two keycards

"Yes," Parson practiced to himself, "I realize that opening two notrump, even with a six-card major is a little unusual. Watch Hereford mangle every hand he declares for a couple of years, and you'd learn to seize every opportunity to open notrump. Lack of a club stopper, does not, and will not, ever bother me. Hereford transferred to hearts and then showed clubs; to me, Blackwood was very appropriate. Four notrump asks for keycards in hearts, and Hereford's five-heart response showed two of them: I presumed the ace of clubs and the king of hearts. Who would think he'd treat the king of clubs as a keycard, although, I guess he took my bid as keycard in *clubs*, the last-bid suit. Nonetheless, I trusted him to have two keycards for hearts so I bid seven. Since this was matchpoints, I would always prefer notrump to hearts." Parson felt this line of argument would appease the most meticulous judge, and he relaxed into his seat to enjoy finessing East-West for a spectacular 2220. West led a diamond against seven notrump, and Parson cava-

223

lierly crossed to dummy at trick two, advancing the heart queen. East followed low, and Parson took the finesse, believing he was playing this hand:

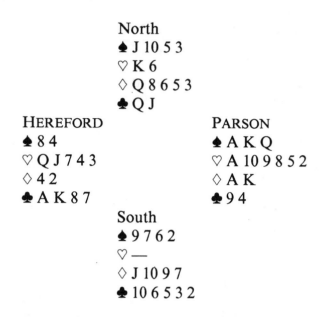

North
♠ J 10 5 3
♡ K 6
♢ Q 8 6 5 3
♣ Q J

HEREFORD
♠ 8 4
♡ Q J 7 4 3
♢ 4 2
♣ A K 8 7

PARSON
♠ A K Q
♡ A 10 9 8 5 2
♢ A K
♣ 9 4

South
♠ 9 7 6 2
♡ —
♢ J 10 9 7
♣ 10 6 5 3 2

The heart finesse was entirely explainable. North had hesitated ever so lightly when the heart queen was led, had he not? Parson read him immediately for the king of hearts. What great table feel Parson had.

But Meyer had arranged for Penny to switch the key card. As Parson was preparing to ride the "proven" finesse into triumphant glory, South, damn her, showed the heart king. The stiff king offside beheaded Parson's finesse, leaving him standing ankle deep in his own blood —minus 100 for a bottom, instead of plus 2220 for seven notrump making seven:

North
♠ J 10 ⑥ 5 3
♡ 6
◇ Q 8 6 5 3
♣ Q J

HEREFORD
♠ 8 4
♡ Q J 7 4 3
◇ 4 2
♣ A K 8 7

PARSON
♠ A K Q
♡ A 10 9 8 5 2
◇ A K
♣ 9 4

South
♠ 9 7 2
♡ Ⓚ
◇ J 10 9 7
♣ 10 6 5 3 2

Parson's spirit expired. He sat: vacant eyes, mouth ajar, skin limp. Parson looked across at Hereford in disbelief. After many years in business, Hereford knew this look well. Parson had started to panic. Now was not the time, Hereford thought, and moved into action. He needed Parson now. "Settle down there, Parson," Hereford's soothing voice lapped at Parson's ears. "It could have happened to anybody," he continued calmly, "Hard to tell where that king was. Let's just play the next hand; it's the last hand of the tournament. Let's dig in," Hereford encouraged.

Boy, Ford thought quietly, *this is the first card Parson's misguessed in three days. Hereford must be really worried; I've certainly never seen him act like this.* Meyer and Penny had done their jobs; switching the spade six for the heart king had produced the desired result.

Like a boxer who had almost gone to the mat, Parson stumbled, picked himself up, stunned and dizzy, and went back in to fight. He would have the last hand. It would be brilliant. His mind, still addled, continued to project: Mother would see the hand plastered across the bridge magazines. She would finally be silenced by his newly acquired fame and respect.

Collecting himself, he took the East cards out of Board 26, the last board of the event:

```
Vul: N-S          North
Dlr: South        ♠ A Q 10 8 4 2
                  ♡ J 10 2
                  ◊ 9
                  ♣ 6 5 2
      HEREFORD                    PARSON
      ♠ 6 5                       ♠ K J
      ♡ K 8 5 3                   ♡ A 9 4
      ◊ 10 7 6 4                  ◊ Q 8 5 3 2
      ♣ Q 10 4                    ♣ K 9 8
                  South
                  ♠ 9 7 3
                  ♡ Q 7 6
                  ◊ A K J
                  ♣ A J 7 3
```

WEST	NORTH	EAST	SOUTH
HEREFORD		PARSON	
—	—	—	1NT
Pass	4♡*	Pass	4♠
Pass	Pass	Pass	
* = transfer			

226

Holding the key cards had a comforting effect on Parson, and he remembered that this, in fact, was going to be an opportunity for a spectacular play. He also recalled that if he was playing against a good South player, that he (in this case, it turned out to be she) would most definitely open a strong notrump. North would then, Parson calculated, transfer into a spade game. As long as Hereford led a club . . .

Hereford dispassionately looked at his hand. Remembering his instructions, he led a club to Parson's king, and declarer's ace. Predictably, declarer started thinking. Parson rested easily in his chair, with the barest hint of a smile floating on his face. Declarer knew there were two heart losers. One of dummy's clubs could go on the top diamonds, but not only would that leave a club loser, it would also leave a potential trump loser, two on a bad day. A good declarer, and this woman was that, would recognize this as an opportunity to combine chances in the spade and diamond suits.

The best line of play is to spurn the trump finesse by playing to the ace, and take a diamond finesse instead. This way, if the diamond finesse wins, both of dummy's club losers are thrown away. If you play the alternative line and take the spade finesse first, you fail to maximize your potential. The diamond finesse gives declarer an additional chance to succeed if the spade king should drop singleton offside. Boiled down to the bones, the question is one of percentages. Does declarer take a simple 50-50 spade finesse, or does she go one better by trying a 50-50 diamond finesse plus the extra chance of a stiff spade king offside. Sure, the diamond finesse might risk an extra undertrick, but most declarers in an aggressive game and already faced with the most damaging

(Repeated for convenience)
Vul: N-S   North
Dlr: South   ♠ A Q 10 8 4 2
          ♡ J 10 2
          ◇ 9
          ♣ 6 5 2

HEREFORD   PARSON
♠ 6 5   ♠ K J
♡ K 8 5 3   ♡ A 9 4
◇ 10 7 6 4   ◇ Q 8 5 3 2
♣ Q 10 4   ♣ K 9 8

      South
     ♠ 9 7 3
     ♡ Q 7 6
     ◇ A K J
     ♣ A J 7 3

opening lead would probably take that risk; Parson was banking on it.

Sure enough, after serious study, declarer played a spade to the ace at trick two; Parson followed with the smoothest king you've ever seen. Parson had a smug smile smeared across his face, knowing declarer would discern the layout of the trump suit as:

         ♠ A Q 10 8 4 2
♠ J 6 5   ♠ K
         ♠ 9 7 3

Parson's mind started to celebrate. Clearly, declarer would think that the diamond finesse was no longer necessary, would cross back to her hand with a high diamond, cash the other high diamond to throw one club loser, and then lead a spade to finesse the 10. That would give declarer 10 easy tricks, losing only one club and two hearts. Parson, who had, in actuality, started the deal with king-jack doubleton of spades, would pounce on the ten with his surprise jack, then cash a fast club and two hard hearts, and beat the "unbeatable" contract.

Winning the event would pale in the brilliant light of his stellar falsecard play. They would call him "Master." This deceptive coup would appear in bridge journals throughout the world. But Parson was counting chickens that would never hatch.

Declarer, upon winning the spade ace, called next for the spade queen. Parson looked up in wonderment, "How could this be?" Baffled, but not beaten, he shook it off. *This dame doesn't realize she should finesse Hereford for the jack.* Slightly embarrassed, Parson followed with the jack and Hereford showed out!

What was going on? Parson's fantasy, doused with a bucket of cold reality, dissolved. Alone and confused, Parson tried to understand what had happened. Parson's intellect reached out tentatively. There had been a switch, or his memory had failed him utterly. Such a small thing; changing the six of spades for the six of hearts. But switching sixes had sealed Parson's fate. The actual deal was:

```
                  North
                  ♠ A Q 10 8 4 2
                  ♡ J 10 2
                  ◊ 9
                  ♣ 6 5 2
HEREFORD                            PARSON
♠ 5                                 ♠ K J
♡ K 8⑥5 3                           ♡ A 9 4
◊ 10 7 6 4                          ◊ Q 8 5 3 2
♣ Q 10 4                            ♣ K 9 8
                  South
                  ♠ 9 7⑥3
                  ♡ Q 7
                  ◊ A K J
                  ♣ A J 7 3
```

229

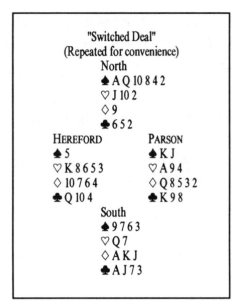

"Switched Deal"
(Repeated for convenience)

North
♠ A Q 10 8 4 2
♡ J 10 2
♦ 9
♣ 6 5 2

HEREFORD
♠ 5
♡ K 8 6 5 3
♦ 10 7 6 4
♣ Q 10 4

PARSON
♠ K J
♡ A 9 4
♦ Q 8 5 3 2
♣ K 9 8

South
♠ 9 7 6 3
♡ Q 7
♦ A K J
♣ A J 7 3

Indeed the declarer *was* an expert. She still had a good reason to combine her spade and diamond chances, and she was rewarded by the astonishing fall of the spade king. She was a bit amused when Parson followed with the jack on the queen; frankly, it surprised her. Why would Parson make such a play? But as declarer was a savvy competitor of the female persuasion, she assumed Parson's cunning. He was probably trying to con her *out* of the diamond finesse, so she *took* it and threw away both of dummy's club losers, making five! Parson and Hereford ought to go into the business of selling goose eggs, Ford thought happily to himself, and sell this big, fat zero. The competitors left Hereford, Parson and Ford sitting at the table. Hereford's tan was looking lavender, his big forehead vein pulsing with his racing heart. Hereford raised his solid body from the chair and barked, "Whose side are you on, anyway? You probably cost us the event! Club lead—phooey! I'll be back. I'm going to find out what in the hell is going on around here."

"Hereford, it wasn't my fault! . . . ." Parson called out. *Oh God, there he goes.* Ford had quietly disappeared. Penny, mini-recorder in pocket, ambled conspicuously outside the bridge room. She wanted to make sure Hereford could easily find her when his indignation was at its peak. She and Meyer had speculated on which would inspire more rage in Hereford, losing the game or being double-crossed. The decision was for the latter. It would be harder on his ego. Out of the side of her eye, she caught the unmistakable image of a runaway freight train hurdling right for her. Reaching into her pocket, she clicked on the machine. He snatched her by the elbow and roughly pushed her out of hearing range of the other players. "You think you can get away with this? You are a stupid, stupid girl. I will ruin you. I will make sure you never work again. Your lovely pictures will be plastered all the way to hell and back! You don't do this to *me*."

"What are you talking about? And get your hands off me now!" Penny did some yelling of her own.

"What am I talking about? Don't talk to me like I'm one of your stupid friends. Parson screwed up those last two hands. The deals were switched. Strangely, you were walking around fooling with the boards. Strangely, those were the only deals that were switched. You'd better plan on moving far away, because I will make it my personal project to ruin your life here." Hereford's invective temporarily finished, he headed back into the room to wait for the scores. Making sure he was well out of sight, Penny slipped her hand back into her pocket and clicked off the small machine.

Finesse

Meyer and Ford stood in the ballroom foyer watching the tight clutch of players swarming around the result board. The head director appeared with computer printout sheets in his hand. As the sheets were posted, a collective gasp swallowed the room. In the wake one lone cry of ecstacy flared like a match in a pitch black cave, "I won! Parson, we won!" Hereford bellowed. The crowd chorused with congratulations, and Hereford cackled with satisfaction. Despite two zeros on the last two boards, Hereford and Parson had won the Blue Ribbon Pairs, the most prestigious pair event in the country.

"Well," Meyer turned to Ford, "looks like there'll be a party tonight."

"Yep. Sure does," Ford replied stonily.

"Will we be attending?" Meyer asked.

"I think I'll be going stag tonight, if you and Penny don't mind missing all the fun," Ford sighed resolutely.

"Not at all, partner," Meyer said, rocking back on his heels.

* * * * * * * * *

Ford slipped through the horde of players and made his way up to his room. Without a doubt Hereford would have a blow-the-roof-off victory celebration, and Ford fully intended to crash that bash. He showered, shaved, and found his most comfortably-worn jeans. He didn't bother to wrap the bottle of Dom Perignon he had purchased from the hotel bar; the label was wrapping enough. He set it on the coffee table.

"Ford, it's us," Meyer called out and rapidly tapped on the door. Ford unlatched the door and smiled at his friends. "Come on in, sit down," he said.

"Ford, this is for you. A token of my friendship," Penny handed Ford a long, white envelope.

He felt the envelope. "The tape?" he asked animatedly.

"A copy of the tape. The League has the original. And you'll be very happy to know that we captured Hereford's self-incrimination with a surprising clarity. His voice just booms," Penny twinkled.

"Are they going to make an announcement revoking the title?" Ford asked.

"Of course. But they decided to wait until the end of the week to make the announcement, to try and minimize the chaos," Penny said easily.

"Hereford should enjoy this, don't you think, guys? He loves the twists and turns in the game of who outsmarted who," Ford said sportingly.

"He'll get a taste of his own medicine. Fitting," Meyer added.

"Ford, Meyer tells me you're going to deprive us of witnessing the victory celebration," Penny said with a note of disappointment.

"I'm afraid so. I've gotta do this one by myself. You know how it is," Ford sighed. "Besides, we don't need Hereford threatening you with any more grief right now."

"We'll get some room service," Penny suggested.

"Good idea. Just make sure you get enough food. I'll take a steak, rare, with all the trimmings." Ford quickly surveyed the room, "Okay, hmm, it looks like I've got everything together here. Champagne, tape . . ."

"Humility, Ford. Where's your humility?" Meyer teased.

"Oh. Right. I lost it in the dryer with one of my socks. It really won't be missed though. Not with Hereford, anyway." Ford grinned roguishly. "I'll be right back," he said, and vanished into the hallway.

* * * * * * * * * *

The elevator doors opened into the opulent hallway that distinguished the VIP floor. The carpet had a deep plush, and the chandeliers dangled casually from the ceiling, sending sparkles dancing over the linen wallpaper. Staring into the Louis-the-something gilt mirror that hung prominently in front of the elevator doors, Ford braced himself, and turned down the hallway and followed the festive din.

It amazed Ford that so many people were willing to be around Hereford. But, he thought, I guess everybody likes a winner. Especially a winner who was throwing a lavishly decadent party, which undoubtedly Hereford was. Ford had arrived, uninvited and unwelcome.

He banged loudly on the door. He counted to sixty and banged again. Eventually the door slowly opened to reveal a striking redhead, glamorously clad except for her long, shapely legs. "Hello," she said pleasantly, offering a creamy smile. "Please come in," she beckoned with her supple hand.

"No, thank you," Ford said with a moment's regret that he was not attending this party. "I'm looking for Hereford. I would like to congratulate him," Ford barely remembered why he was here.

"Well, why don't you come in?" she questioned.

"Uh," he stuttered. *That's a good question*, he thought to himself. "I'm his son," Ford slapped his mind, "and I have to play bridge in the morning. I just wanted to—"

"Ooo, his *son*. I didn't know he *had* a son. Let me get him." She pressed herself through the throng of partiers.

Ford waited patiently in the doorway, the invisible guest.

Hereford stepped boldly through the crowd, chest first. "Yes?" he said impatiently.

"I came to say congratulations. I brought you these." Ford offered the champagne and the sealed envelope containing the tape. "Congratulations again, on your win," Ford demurred.

"Thank you," said Hereford, and coldly closed the door.

"You're welcome," Ford said to the door.

* * * * * * * * *

With the lightness of a man who has just had casts removed from both legs, Ford Maddox, having excised the twin tumors of Vanessa and Hereford in the same week, blissfully started back to his room, and the warmth of his friends. He was already planning the resurrection of Richie's club, Aces. As he thought about the coming weeks, he savored the prospect of spending time with his favorite threesome: Penny, Richie and Meyer. He hadn't won a single masterpoint, but this was turning out to be the most satisfying nationals of his career.

The Final Trade-Off

Half-asleep, Maura unsteadily picked up an incessantly-ringing phone. It was Monday morning, 9 a.m., and she could still hear airplane engines whirring and feel airplane germs floating inside her bedroom. "Maura!" Prissy screamed into the phone, "I just heard a radio report that some local bridge stars have been implicated in a major cheating scandal at the Chicago Nationals. I can't believe we left right before all the excitement started. I know one of the director's mothers, and I've got the whole story. I have a brilliant plan. I'll tell you everything when I pick you up later for our game."

* * * * * * * * * *

The club was its usual 40 degrees. But that was the only aspect that was usual. For one thing, Eileen hadn't yet made a single foray to the food counter. She and all the other girls were crowded around Maura and Prissy who were holding court in the center of the large room.

Maura, faithful to Prissy's plan, was silent except for a small (but noticeably dramatic) cough. She listened with greater fascination than the other ladies as Priscilla spoke. Maura knew more about what was going on than the others, and so, was even more appreciative of Prissy's emerging skills at weaving fantasy out of fact.

"Let me tell you all about it, girls," Prissy was saying. "First, poor Maura got the unsettling news from the surgeon that her specific condition might have to be treated by a specialist in atomic medicine. I was sitting right next to the poor dear in the office as the doctor discussed the micro-surgery." Maura drank in the pitying and marveling glances as a desert-wanderer drinks his first sip of water after 30 years without liquid.

"In order to try and cheer her up," Prissy continued, beautifully working the room, "I made sure we had kibitzing seats at the Blue Ribbons. We were right in the middle of the whole thing. Why, it was while we were kibitzing Mr. Willis and that Parson person that the directors first started to notice something. Here's how it happened . . ."

Other Natco Press Bridge Books

To Bid or Not to Bid (The Law of Total Tricks)
    by Larry Cohen   ..... $12.95 ea.

Following the Law
    by Larry Cohen   ..... $12.95 ea.

Bridge My Way
    by Zia Mahmood   ..... $12.95 ea.

Everyone's Guide to the
<u>New</u> Convention Card
    by Marty Bergen   ..... $9.95 ea.

Also Available

Better Bidding with Bergen (Vol. I)
    Uncontested Auctions
    by Marty Bergen   ..... $11.95 ea.

Better Bidding with Bergen (Vol. II)
    Contested Auctions
    by Marty Bergen   ..... $9.95 ea.

Points Schmoints (Hardcover)
    By Marty Bergen   ..... $19.95 ea.

To order any of these books please send check (U.S. funds only) or money order (**add $3.00 postage/handling**) to:

Natco Press
10481 Milburn Lane
Boca Raton, FL 33498

About the Authors

Larry Cohen is one of America's leading bridge players and the holder of 16 national championships. His first book, *To Bid or Not to Bid*, was the best-selling bridge book of the 1990's.

Liz Davis is pursuing a graduate degree at NYU. She spends her free time with her dogs, her motorcycle, and her husband Steve Weinstein, one of the country's top bridge players.

To order additional copies of this book, send $12.95 per copy + $3.00 P/H to the address on the preceding page.

For information on the ACBL (American Contract Bridge League) call toll-free 1-800-467-1623